ANNA ALCOTT

Mexican Interlude

Copyright © 2024 by Anna Alcott

All rights reserved. No part of this publication may be reproduced, stored or transmitted in any form or by any means, electronic, mechanical, photocopying, recording, scanning, or otherwise without written permission from the publisher. It is illegal to copy this book, post it to a website, or distribute it by any other means without permission.

First edition

*This book was professionally typeset on Reedsy.
Find out more at reedsy.com*

Contents

Acknowledgement	v
1	1
2	5
3	13
4	18
5	25
6	33
7	44
8	60
9	68
10	71
11	79
12	88
13	94
14	98
15	107
16	111
17	118
18	126
19	130
20	140
21	143
22	153
23	157

24	167
25	180
26	189
27	196
28	206
29	211
30	219
31	224
32	230
About the Author	239
Also by Anna Alcott	240

Acknowledgement

Thanks to all my friends from various writing groups. To Amalia, who encouraged me to keep writing; to Ceci and Tracy, who provided invaluable, tough criticism; and a BIG thank you to Simone Gredel for saving my sanity when designing the book cover. To my darling Jessica, who inspired the character of Olivia. All your support and insights have been indispensable.
I also have to mention Reedsy.com. It's a great writing platform and the customer service is outstanding.

A note to readers: *While some towns in this book bear real names, the geography is not depicted with complete accuracy. I've taken artistic license to serve the story.*

On a personal note, I have had articles and short stories printed in various magazines. This my first novel, with two more in progress. If you enjoyed it, please leave a review.

Check out my website: www.annaalcott.com
or FB Page: Writers Forum PT
Any comments: annaalcott@gmail.com

1

In a non-descript warehouse on the outskirts of Los Angeles, DEA (Drug Enforcement Administration) agent Juan Carlos Castillo crouched behind a large shipping container. The pain in his knee, a constant reminder of an old football injury, was becoming unbearable. He gave a small groan as he changed position. It seemed to echo through the air, and he could only hope it hadn't been heard. There was a sudden loud bang, followed by shouting and some kind of chaos. Castillo raised his head just high enough to see that the cause of all the noise was a small packing crate that had fallen and burst open. The smell of Tequila filled the air from the smashed bottles on the floor. He sank down, relieved that the gun in his hand would not be needed—yet.

There was no doubt his situation was dangerous. His confidential informant, a CI he trusted, had reported that the suspects were abandoning the warehouse. With them, they were taking valuable evidence that was extremely important to the case the agency had been building for the past two years.

He had called for backup, and they were on their way, but the situation was deteriorating rapidly. His immediate reaction was to move in alone. He had a reputation for ignoring the rules and doing things his own way. His relentless pursuit of Don

Manuel Vittorio de Costa was coming down to this moment. However, Don Manuel rarely left Mexico, so one of his guys would have to strike a deal with the DEA. Castillo already knew who the weak link was.

Don Manuel was entrenched in one of the largest drug cartels in Mexico. On the surface, his business operated under the guise of a legitimate export company specializing in shipping the finest Mexican Tequila to various countries worldwide. However, in reality, they generated millions from the trafficking of drugs and possibly arms, cleverly concealed within their shipments. It was suspected that one of the many people on his payroll must have been within the customs department. How else would they be able to continue their illicit operations? However, what fueled his deep-seated hatred for Don Manuel was that he had been responsible for the death of his partner one month ago.

Castillo and his partner Jonesy had a bond that extended far beyond their professional lives—they were practically family. Growing up together in the same neighborhood, they attended high school, college, and, eventually, the police academy side by side. They swiftly ascended through the ranks and were eventually recruited to join the DEA, eager to take on the challenges of undercover work. They were both admired and respected by their colleagues, and they were great fun to be with. The ladies loved them.

Jonesy got the first assignment when he infiltrated Don Manuel's cartel. In the world of undercover agents, personal lives ceased to exist.

Castillo missed his friend. One evening, sitting alone in their favorite bar, he had met a woman who turned out to be the love of his life. She was different from most women he had known. They only spent a few months together, and in that time, they fell deeply in love, which meant going undercover was no longer a priority for him. He had even thought about changing careers and starting a family with her.

However, when Jonesy was killed, Castillo's priorities shifted and he made the decision to join the investigation. There wasn't enough time to go undercover, but he spent every minute of both his working and private lives watching or following Manuel's men.

It had happened so quickly, and he wasn't even allowed to tell anyone the truth.

"I've been called away on business. I'm not sure how long I'll be gone," he had told his new girlfriend. He also promised to call her. However, any form of communication that could jeopardize the mission or compromise safety was strictly prohibited. He would truly miss her, but the sacrifice was small as he was determined to avenge his fallen partner and friend.

Once this ordeal concluded, he saw a future with his new love, a fresh chapter filled with shared dreams. He yearned for the day when they could finally embrace the beginning of their journey together.

He thought about his friend and partner, Jonesy. He had been a dedicated undercover agent, but one mistake had sealed his fate—he had become entangled with Maria, Don Manuel's cousin. When Castillo found out, he warned his friend but the romance was discovered, leading to a swift and tragic demise.

Backup still hadn't arrived, and the cartel members were preparing to leave. He knew he couldn't allow this to happen. He needed to stop them now, or all his hard work would be in vain.

Without any warning, a bullet whizzed past him, creating

a distinct shock wave pattern as it sliced through the air, narrowly missing him. Adrenaline surged through his body as he realized he had been spotted. Bullets continued to fly perilously close, and he did his best to avoid them. *Why had he not worn a bullet-proof vest?*

His skin tingled with fear, and sweat made his shirt cling to his body like a wet suit. A red, pea-sized dot appeared, hovering over his chest, and bullets followed one after another. Panic set in as he gasped for air and clawed at his throat, struggling to breathe. Blood seeped from between the buttons of his blue cotton shirt, soaking the fabric.

His vision blurred. He could no longer focus. A warm wetness trickled down his legs. It was blood—his own blood. His body felt strangely light, and instead of pain, a burning, aggravating sensation took over. Tears welled up as he thought of his beautiful girlfriend and the life they had dreamed of together. In those final moments, Castillo clung to the memories of her, sad that she would never learn the truth, and that was perhaps the most painful part of all as his consciousness faded away.

2

Something creaked across the dimly lit hallway as she tightened her grip on the Colt Diamondback. She wasn't easily frightened, but she could feel the gun slip in her hand, slick with sweat. That worried her. If she had to fire the thing, she didn't need it flailing around in her hand like the snake it had been named after."

Sarah gripped the book as her eyes traveled across the pages. She had found it on a chair at the Los Angeles airport. Normally, she didn't read lurid crime fiction, but this mysterious plot did intrigue her. It was something to take her mind off things while treating herself to a well-deserved holiday for her thirtieth birthday. Two weeks of relaxation in a lovely quiet town just outside of Mexico City.

She had slept very little the night before, so the words on the pages quickly became blurred. Her tired eyes slowly closed, and she slipped into a daydream about the time she had spent together with John. Why did she keep thinking about him? It did not end well. It was easier to remember the good times they had together. She had fallen head over heels after only knowing him for a short while.

Sarah's memories of their first encounter brought a warm smile to her face. She recalled how a seemingly dull conference lecture had driven her to seek refuge in the bar, where a chance meeting had changed the course of her life. The recollection of that night's events brought a mix of embarrassment and gratitude to Sarah's thoughts. Yes, those gin and tonics, coupled with her empty stomach, had indeed taken their toll on her balance and judgment. The lack of food and the alcohol had left her feeling woozy, and she had nearly tumbled off the bar stool. It was then that the stranger had come to her rescue, his quick reflexes preventing what could have been a rather embarrassing fall.

"Are you okay?" he asked as he held out his hand.

"I am, thank you," she said to the dark-haired man.

"Can I buy you a drink, or should I suggest a coffee?" he said with a slight smirk.

Sarah's face reddened. "A cappuccino would go down well."

Their conversation had flowed effortlessly, punctuated by laughter and shared stories. She had felt a connection with him, a spark that was impossible to ignore. As the evening wore on, the stranger's company had been so enjoyable that time had slipped away unnoticed, and her body's fatigue had finally caught up with her in the form of a giant yawn. Their parting had been filled with both reluctance and promise. She had accepted his business card with a smile, and tucked it safely in her bag, knowing there would be many future dinner dates. Sarah had returned to her hotel room that night, replaying their conversation and contemplating the possibility of a new beginning.

That was how it all began. They were both busy individuals, she with her agency and John with his IT clients, but they had managed to spend a lot of time together. Was it lust or love? She hoped the latter. After five months, he had suggested that they take a mini cruise on one of his friend's private yachts.

Sarah was glad that she had left England, as her travel business in California had become very successful due to hard work and dedication. Her brief but valuable experience with Virgin Airlines had allowed her to establish a network of affluent clients who valued her personalized services over online alternatives. So, she deserved a break and trusted her assistant Anne to look after the business while she was gone.

Sailing around the Caribbean had been nothing short of exhilarating. Together, they had explored picturesque towns in Jamaica, the Bahamas, and the Cayman Islands, the turquoise waters and the warm Caribbean breeze forming the backdrop to their budding romance. She had found her soulmate, someone who shared her love for exploration and adventure.

Well, that's what she thought until they had returned to Los Angeles. She pushed all thoughts from her mind and laid back to relax. The passenger in the next seat introduced herself.

"Hi, my name's Susan."

"Hi, I'm Sarah. Pleased to meet you."

Sarah welcomed a distraction from the thoughts of John and asked, "How long are you planning to stay in Mexico?"

"I'm visiting my sister, and she wants me to live there permanently to be close to her children. But before I make that decision, I thought I'd take a couple of months to explore and see how I like it."

Sarah responded warmly, "That sounds like a wonderful plan. Mexico is a beautiful place to be, and I'm sure you'll enjoy your time here."

"What about all the problems with drugs?"

"Well," said Sarah, "I've been told that while drugs can be found in any city, the real problems are concentrated mainly along the US/Mexico border. We certainly have issues in the US too, so it's not just isolated to one country."

"You sound very knowledgeable. Do you travel a lot?"

Sarah nodded. "Yes, traveling is a big part of my job as a travel agent. I get to explore many different places."

As the conversation flowed, Susan let out a yawn. "Excuse me," she said, "it's been a long day. I need another nap."

I wish I could sleep on a plane, thought Sarah. She recalled the conversation she just had and realized how lucky Susan was to have a wonderful, caring family. Sarah's family history was marked by estrangement and difficult circumstances. Her biological mother had abandoned her when she was five years old, and her father, plagued by alcoholism, was unable to provide a stable home. So, they lived with his mother, who took care of her during her early years.

Her grandmother, while providing shelter, was not a loving presence. She had her own struggles, particularly with Sarah's father, who was often found in a drunken stupor, with an ashtray overflowing with cigarette butts. One fateful day, her father's recklessness led to a small fire when he fell asleep with a burning cigarette. Fearing for Sarah's safety, authorities decided to place her in a foster home when she was only seven. It was there that she found the warmth and care of a family who treated her as their own, showering her with affection and providing the peace and tranquility that she had so often craved. On her eighteenth birthday, while at home alone, a knock on the front door shattered the tranquility of the household. A policeman stood there, his expression somber, casting a shadow over what should have been a day of celebration and joy.

"Are you Sarah Houghton?"

"Yes."

2

"I'm sorry, miss, but there's been a terrible accident!"

Sarah fell back against the wall. Both her foster parents had been killed in a car crash.

So, as her father was in jail and her grandmother had passed, she was now completely alone.

Through many failed relationships, she wondered if she would ever settle down. She often considered adopting a child, even if she was without a partner. Sarah sighed and thought about her relationship with John. They were doing great until the day he had ghosted her. Now, she was more angry than worried. How could he just not call or text? They had spent the most wonderful time together. What a fool she had been. For her, it had been something special, but now she realized it maybe had been just a fling for him. What if he was married? Maybe that is why when they had returned to Los Angeles, they hadn't spent much time together. However, after one month, she had been pleasantly surprised when John finally invited her to meet his friends, as he was usually vague about his private life. She had dressed carefully. She had wanted to look her best to make a good first impression. The phone rang.

"Sarah, I'm so sorry, but I've been called away on a business trip."

"Okay, I understand. Work comes first."

"I should only be gone for a few days. I'll call as soon as I get back, I promise."

As a freelance IT expert, he was often called away to sort out client's computer and network issues. Sarah often asked him exactly what he did. He would joke, "I'm a spy," then laugh, "Seriously, it's too technical for me to explain."

Suddenly, the plane lurched and brought Sarah back to the present. Susan woke up startled and grabbed Sarah's arm. "Oh my God!" she shouted. "Are we crashing?"

"Don't worry, it's only turbulence," replied Sarah gently.

The flight attendant's soothing voice came through the speaker. "Ladies and gentlemen, the captain has requested that you should please fasten your seat belts. Just a little turbulence, so the ride will be a little bumpy for the next few minutes. Nothing to worry about."

Susan sat back and gulped down her drink. Sarah's mind wandered back to John. Six days after he had left, Sarah still had not heard from him, and she was worried. No phone call, no text. She realized she had no contact information for his friends or family, so she had no idea how to find him. What if something had happened to him? She had pushed back her tears and had grabbed her phone. There were four hospitals, and she had called them all. She got the same answer, "Sorry, ma'am, there's no one here with that name."

Another day passed with no contact from him, so she decided to file a missing person's report. Before that happened, she received a text from him.

'Sorry, babe. Something came up. I'll call you in a couple of days'.

That couple of days turned into weeks, then months. Sarah decided that the best way to free herself from this emotional limbo was to take a real holiday, one filled with sunshine, laughter, and the laid-back lifestyle of the Mexican people. It was a chance to rediscover herself, to bask in the warmth of the sun and the vibrant culture of Mexico, hoping it would help her find clarity and peace of mind.

However, a nagging thought persisted. She recalled the stories John had once shared about his own trip south of the border, not too far from where she was heading. It seemed like an absurd notion, but what if he was in Mexico, too? What if, by some twist of fate, they crossed paths once again? Would she be angry with him for disappearing or overjoyed to see him once more?

Sarah looked out the window. The sky was a bright blue above the carpet of fluffy white clouds. She leaned back in the soft leather seat, her auburn hair spread about her shoulders. She sighed and ordered a martini.

The final hour of the flight remained tranquil and uneventful. The flight attendant's announcement came, "Ladies and gentlemen, please fasten your seat belts and put your tray in an upright position."

The landing gear vibrated through the cabin, and Sarah's ears popped as the cabin pressure normalized. Mexico City appeared below, a place she had visited numerous times on business trips. However, this time, it was different. This trip was meant for pure relaxation and enjoyment.

The plane glided smoothly to a landing, and after a short taxi, it came to a complete stop. Sarah bid farewell to Susan and stepped off the plane into the sweltering heat and humidity of Mexico City. It was three days before Christmas. This holiday was the best Christmas present she could have given herself. She had never been one for traditional Christmases. With no family, no children, and her vegetarian lifestyle that made turkey unappealing, she preferred to celebrate the season in her own unique way.

Sarah's prescription glasses automatically darkened to shield her eyes from the bright sun as she crossed the scorching tarmac and entered the crowded airport, with travelers from various corners of the world. The lines at customs and immigration seemed to snake endlessly, but Sarah managed to secure a spot near the front, with only five people ahead of her.

"*Pasaporte, por favor*," said the somber agent.

"Of course." Sarah handed him the document. He glanced through the heavily stamped, dog-eared pages.

"This is not an American passport. Do you have your green card?"

"Yes, sir," she said and flashed it in front of him.

"You travel a lot, *senorita.*"

"Yes, I'm a travel agent."

"Thank you. Have a good stay," he said in perfect English.

Sixty hot, bumpy minutes later, a sweating Sarah climbed off the airport shuttle bus, checked into the Las Brisas hotel, and went up to her room.

Refreshed by a cool shower, she stood on the balcony and admired the spectacular view. A thousand miles of coastline touched the Gulf of Mexico to the west and north, and the Caribbean to the east.

Sarah's hotel was nestled in the charming old fishing town of Costa del Luna. While it held only a three-star rating, it was a favorite among European guests who appreciated its authenticity and tranquility. Unlike the bustling and more touristy resort of Isla de Mexico a few miles away, which was preferred by many Americans for its upscale restaurants and world-class golf course. She planned to visit the upscale resort to explore its potential as a destination for her special clients. Despite it being overpriced for her budget, she could certainly appreciate its beauty and appeal to certain clientele.

As she settled into her hotel, Sarah looked forward to exploring the authentic charm of the fishing town. Her holiday promised to be a perfect blend of relaxation and exploration, all under the warm Mexican sun.

3

Sarah's hunger led her downstairs to the hotel's dining room, where the aroma of garlic hung in the air, and the dining room buzzed with activity. Waiters moved swiftly, seeming to navigate the chaos with an apparent disorganization, but no one seemed to mind the wait. After all, everyone was here to relax and enjoy their vacation.

Sarah studied and admired the local artwork adorning every wall. The bright colors and cheerful scenes of beaches and fishermen added to the ambiance of the restaurant. The maître d' approached her, explaining that due to the dinner rush, the wait for a table might exceed an hour. He asked if she would mind sharing a table with some other English guests. Sarah, her hunger taking precedence, readily agreed. The waiter led her to a table occupied by five people near a large window that offered a picturesque view of the bay. Among them was a red-haired, pale-faced Englishman dressed impeccably in a beige suit and tie. *But who wears a tie in this heat?* Sarah couldn't help but find his choice of attire a bit peculiar, given the sweltering temperatures, but she appreciated his good manners as he pulled out a chair for her.

She estimated he was around thirty-five. He was slender, and his unkempt hair occasionally fell across his face, partially concealing a scar on his forehead. His voice carried a commanding edge, hinting at the possibility of military experience. She introduced herself.

"Nice to meet you. My name's Harry Whelan, and this is James and Jonathan." The two waved, then continued with what sounded like a heated political discussion. Harry dismissed them and pointed to the young couple at the end of the table. "Edward and Margaret are newlyweds and unaware of anyone else."

"Nice to meet you all," said Sarah, knowing none of them had heard her.

"We were all at uni together and decided to have a reunion. So, how long are you staying here?" Harry asked Sarah.

"Two weeks, maybe three. It depends on whether my assistant can handle my business on her own."

Throughout their conversation, she noticed Harry looking over her shoulder as if he were expecting someone. Sarah found this habit extremely rude and couldn't help but feel a bit annoyed by it. Harry's behavior took a somewhat abrupt turn when he summoned a passing waiter, giving orders for more coffee and water. Due to his curt manner, Sarah's initial impression of him began to shift slightly. He could be a little more polite, she thought.

He shifted the conversation, asking, "So, do you visit Mexico often?" His inquiry seemed genuine, and Sarah appreciated the opportunity to discuss her fondness for the country and her experiences there. The waiter took her order and she scoffed the food down quickly, as it was the first meal she had eaten all day. She never ordered plane food, so usually carried a couple of protein bars and a packet of nuts.

Sarah noticed the arrival of tempting desserts just as she

was about to leave the table. The sight of chocolate mousse, lemon meringue, and Mexican custards proved too tempting to resist. She decided to indulge, making a silent promise to double her exercise routine during her stay to offset the extra calories. Sarah ordered a Mexican custard and savored each bite, thoroughly enjoying the sweet treat. On her last mouthful, a voice said,

"Hello, chaps, sorry I'm late."

"Oh, Charles, old boy, there you are. Sarah, last but not least, this is the ugly bug in our crowd, Charles Benson."

Sarah looked up and stared into his large, blue eyes and noticed the casual style of his thick, black, hair. She gracefully wiped her mouth.

Charles, with a charming smile, touched her chin. "You missed a bit of custard."

Sarah, somewhat flustered, carefully wiped it away and shook hands with Charles, feeling his grip linger longer than expected. She quickly pulled her hand away and decided it was time to depart.

What is it with guys? she thought. Probably thinks due to his good looks, women will fawn all over him. "Nice meeting you all," Sarah said politely, "But I need to go. It's been a long day." She made her way through the crowded dining room, aware of those blue eyes watching her leave. Navigating the bustling restaurant, Sarah almost collided with a waiter before bumping into a tall man near the door. She stammered an apology, but the man touched her arm briefly, preventing her from knocking over a nearby vase. He offered her a playful smile and asked, "Why are you in such a hurry, *senorita*? This is Mexico, a place to relax and enjoy life." With those words, he disappeared into the lively bar, leaving Sarah standing there, slightly dazed by the unexpected encounters of two handsome men.

The fatigue from the day finally caught up with her, and she welcomed the chance to rest and rejuvenate, knowing that her Mexican adventure had only just begun.

Charles Benson watched Sarah's departure, finding her incredibly attractive with an enviable figure. He entertained the hope of having a few evenings out on the town with her, though he sensed a guarded quality about her. Perhaps it was the aftermath of a difficult relationship or breakup. This reaction was unusual for Charles, who typically maintained a more aloof demeanor. He couldn't pinpoint whether it was her alluring cologne or the graceful sway of her hips that had captivated him.

However, Charles had to remind himself that his presence in this small beach town was primarily for business, not romance. He knew he'd have to keep any potential encounters casual and maintain the facade of a tourist.

He had been invited on this reunion with old friends from university. He hadn't seen them for a few years and was mainly curious to see how they had turned out. It was also a good excuse to mix pleasure with business.

Harry, who had been indulging in shots of Tequila, urged Charles to join in. Charles declined, knowing Tequila wasn't to his taste, and instead requested a double Scotch to satisfy his palate. His thoughts kept returning to Sarah, and he couldn't shake the strong attraction he had felt within moments of meeting her. She appeared sophisticated yet retained a childlike quality that intrigued him. Typically, such attractions were uncommon for him, but the extended period without companionship left him wondering if perhaps he was grappling with a bout of sexual frustration. He made a mental note to find her at breakfast the next day, wondering if she was an early riser or someone who enjoyed sleeping in. He sat chatting with his old mates, yet it appeared that they didn't share as much common ground as he had with them all those years ago. He knocked back a couple of Scotches, then said goodbye to the crowd who were slowly getting drunker and drunker. They haven't changed in all these years, thought Charles as he made his way to his room.

4

Sarah woke with the sun streaming through the shutters, revealing the scattered bed covers, victims of a humid night. She took a long shower then went down for breakfast. After perusing the menu, she ordered *Huevos Rancheros*, mild. To her dismay, the chef's idea of mild was certainly not hers. Choking and spluttering, Sarah grabbed her glass of water as a familiar voice asked, "Are you okay?" Charles stood over her.

"Yes," she gasped as she gulped down the remaining water.

"May I join you?"

"Of course," she replied, pointing to the seat next to her. This was her chance to find out whether his good looks were his only attribute. Many handsome men often relied solely on their looks and lacked personality. However, she needed to show him that she was certainly not ready for a holiday romance. In the back of her mind, she still thought that John may show up at her doorstep one day. Their love had been real—or so she had thought.

The waiter came by and took Charles' order. Sarah observed him as he sipped his coffee and hoped that he did not want to delve into her past. Sarah didn't like talking about herself.

But it was inevitable as Charles asked, "So, do I detect a slight Northern accent?"

"Yes, I'm a bit of a chameleon. I once lived with two gals from Texas. You should have heard me then."

"God forbid," Charles quipped, laughing.

Sarah replied in a comically bad Texan drawl, "Well, I'll be."

Charles leaned back in his chair and shared a bit of his background, "As you probably guessed, I went to public boarding school. I hated it with a passion and couldn't wait to leave. My parents came from a wealthy family, but they made their own money from real estate and thought boarding school would give me the best education there was."

The exchange was light-hearted, and Sarah appreciated the ease with which they were conversing, even if usually the topic of her past remained firmly off-limits. She found herself gradually opening up to the intriguing man sitting across from her, their conversation taking on a natural flow that made her feel unexpectedly comfortable. As she glanced away, she spotted the stranger that she had almost knocked over the previous evening. He sat at a table across the room, giving him a perfect view of her and Charles. He raised his glass of orange juice and smiled. She tilted her head graciously and smiled back. Charles glared at the man who dared to distract Sarah and said, "One of your typical Romeos, I suspect."

"Don't be silly," she retorted, "Latinos are very friendly people."

"Sure."

"That remark made you sound like a racist," Sarah said sharply.

"I'm sorry, just a twinge of jealousy," he said.

Was he joking? They hardly knew each other. Was he the possessive type?

Sarah changed the subject. "So, I know you are from London

or somewhere close."

"A small town near Southampton, actually. My parents moved from London for a more peaceful existence. Back in those days, the commute to London wasn't half bad. Not like today, too many bloody cars."

Sarah agreed, remembering her last trip to London. "So much traffic, noise, and dirt, but Los Angeles is worse. That's why I live and work in Long Beach, which is about forty-five minutes from downtown Los Angeles - on a good day."

"So where did you say you were born?"

"I didn't. I was born in a small town up north, but my family moved around a lot," she lied.

"Military?"

"No, I..." before she could finish her sentence, Charles' mobile phone rang.

Saved by the bell, thought Sarah.

"Excuse me." He looked at the caller ID, then said, "I'm sorry, I must go. Look, it's Christmas Eve tomorrow night. How about we meet for dinner about nine?"

After a second's hesitation, she replied, "Why not?"

"Breakfast's on me," he said as he rose, leaving a generous amount of pesos on the table and continued his call until he was out of sight.

While the waiter refilled her coffee cup, Sarah felt an unexpected craving for a cigarette. She had quit smoking just before meeting John, though she had succumbed to temptation on a few occasions. Sarah dug into her bag, gathered some pesos, and purchased a pack of Mexican special cigarettes from a nearby vending machine. From the smell, they would probably kill her before she could quit. She took out her lighter, admiring the small piece of gold which was engraved with the initials

J.F. It had belonged to her foster dad, the coincidence being that his last name was Foster. Even if Sarah stopped smoking completely, the lighter would always be with her.

"May I join you?" She looked up to see the handsome stranger.

"Of course," she replied, admiring his dark features, the nose jutting, the lines deep—a face marked by hard living or too much sun.

He introduced himself, "My name is Ricardo, Ricardo Victor Sanchez," with a hint of hesitation.

"Hi, I'm Sarah Houghton."

Two waiters approached the table. Ricardo whispered to them in rapid Spanish, which Sarah couldn't comprehend. The waiters promptly dispersed, leaving a sense of intrigue in the air.

"Great service in here, or are you just an excellent tipper?" said Sarah.

He shook his head and laughed, "Do you speak Spanish?"

"A little, but I am fluent in Italian and speak a little French."

"Well, you shouldn't have any trouble learning Spanish." After a short pause, he asked, "So, that gentleman earlier; is he a good friend?"

"Oh, no. I just met him yesterday." She sipped her coffee and took a puff on her cigarette, inhaled deeply and relished the subtle burn in her chest. The nicotine brought an instant sense of calm.

Ricardo observed her and remarked, "You looked like you enjoyed that."

Sarah nodded, replying, "Yes, I did. It's my first one in quite a few months."

He leaned a little closer. She breathed in his dark, musky

aroma. "That's a lovely gold lighter you have."

"Yes, it belonged to my foster dad.

"Past tense?" remarked Ricardo.

"Both he and my foster mom were killed in a car accident when I was eighteen, actually on my eighteenth birthday."

Ricardo sipped on his water then said, "So, how are you enjoying your vacation? Do you intend to travel around and see some of our wonderful sights?"

"Yes, I have lots of brochures. I can't wait to visit some of the ruins."

He talked about the area and the most interesting sights to see. His baritone, sexy voice mesmerized Sarah. After two cups of coffee, he glanced at his watch. "I apologize. I must go. But if you are free this evening, would you meet me for dinner and I can advise you on all the best places to visit?"

"That's very kind of you," replied Sarah.

"No problem, I'll pick you up outside the hotel at eight." He held out his hand, and as Sarah placed hers in it, he surprised her by kissing it. Watching him leave, she wondered if the gesture, was romantic or just plain corny?

Her heart beat a little faster and she couldn't decide whether it was from the attention of two extremely attractive but different men, or all the coffee she had consumed. It was definitely too early to start a relationship, and she wasn't into holiday romances, so she would just enjoy male companionship. All through her life, she'd had more male friends than female, and some of them weren't even gay.

She and John had discussed starting a family. She knew she was ready for motherhood and she had even set a personal deadline: if she wasn't in a serious relationship within the next year, she would consider adopting, but the first step would be to apply to become a foster mom.

It was a glorious day, so the rest of the morning was spent on the beach, people watching and eating lunch in a local restaurant. She came across a small cafe, called *La Casa de Amigos,* and chatted to the owners who were from Atlanta and spoke with that smooth southern American accent. It was the old part of town where houses lined the cobblestone streets and vibrant bougainvillea spilled over garden walls. As Sarah sat talking with the clientele, who were mainly American, the air was thick with the rich aroma of freshly brewed coffee and the tantalizing scent of homemade tamales. After ten years of living there, they knew all the local gossip. Sarah listened intently.

"Did you hear about Elena from the market?" said Jane, an over tanned blonde. Her sunhat cast a shadow over her face, adding an air of mystery to her words. "They say she's been seen sneaking into the old Rivera mansion late at night."

Tom, a retired professor with a penchant for local history, raised an eyebrow. "The Rivera mansion? That place has been abandoned for years. Why on earth would she go there?"

Susan, who prided herself on being the town's unofficial news correspondent, chimed in. "Word is, she's meeting a secret lover. Some say it's one of the Rivera heirs, come back to claim his family's fortune."

Jane shook her head, "No, no, it's much juicier than that. I heard it's a treasure hunt! There's supposed to be a hidden stash of gold left behind by Pancho Villa himself."

The group fell silent for a moment, each person lost in their own thoughts about the possibilities of the idea of hidden treasure.

"But what about the noises people have been hearing at

night?" asked Tom, breaking the silence. "Strange sounds, like footsteps and whispers. Some say the place is haunted."

Susan laughed, "That's just the cover story, Tom. The real scoop is that Elena is part of a secret society trying to uncover the mansion's mysteries. They've been decoding old letters and maps, and they're close to finding something big."

As the conversation ebbed and flowed, Sarah wondered if they knew anything about Ricardo, but didn't care to ask. Whether it was secret lovers, hidden treasure, or ghostly apparitions, one thing was certain: life in this little Mexican town was anything but dull.

Sarah finished her second coffee and said her goodbyes. She strolled along the boardwalk, buying gifts and souvenirs for friends back home, then returned to the hotel late afternoon and took a nap.

5

Sarah was usually on time for appointments, but she found herself embracing the relaxed *mañana* attitude of Mexico. She had made the right choice coming here on holiday. It was a chance to leave behind worries, problems, and the company of unhappy or negative people. Life felt wonderful.

She was ten minutes late meeting Ricardo because she had phoned her assistant, Anne, to make sure all was going smoothly. Anne reassured her that all was well and mentioned that Mrs. Carter was presently stationed at her desk. A wry smile danced across Sarah's lips as she couldn't help but empathize with Anne. Mrs. Carter was known for her demanding nature. Fortunately, the compensation in the form of commissions from her three annual cruises softened the challenging client interactions.

Ricardo was waiting for her at the hotel entrance. The smile on his suntanned face lit up as Sarah walked toward him. She could see by the look on his face that he was impressed with her elegant white, tight-fitting dress, which showed off her newly acquired tan.

Typically opting for long dresses or trousers, she concealed scars on her legs from a bad fall she suffered a few years ago. Also, she had been unsuccessful in shedding those few extra pounds before leaving the US; now she imagined putting on more if she continued accepting dinner dates.

Ricardo took her by the arm and escorted her to a beige Lexus sports car, an unusual sight in this part of the country.

"I managed to get one when the dealership opened last year. This is my only vice."

Sarah noticed the pride in his face and said jokingly, "Are you sure?"

They laughed as they climbed into the car. Sarah gently caressed the plush leather seats, which she imagined would be very comfortable on a long drive. The dashboard boasted a sophisticated and contemporary design, showcasing a touch-screen for navigation and entertainment control.

Inquisitive about Sarah's musical preferences, Ricardo inquired, "What genre do you enjoy?"

Without missing a beat, she quipped, "The sound system here could make even rap sound good."

Ricardo shot her a sidelong glance.

"Just kidding! I appreciate all music except for rap."

He responded to her eclectic taste, as he tuned into a classical melody, maintaining the volume at a level so they could still carry on a conversation.

Ricardo drove with the skill and confidence of a seasoned driver as they raced down a coastal road. He handled the car with ease, expertly maneuvering around corners and shifting gears effortlessly. Soon, he turned off the main street, and the Lexus purred as they ascended the narrow, winding streets. Along the way, they passed a mix of small, weathered houses interspersed with the occasional mansion—remnants of a more affluent era.

Sarah didn't mind the wind tousling her auburn hair as they

sped along. She took in a deep breath and marveled at the view of the approaching sunset. The warm breeze, the scenic drive, and Ricardo's company made the journey even more enjoyable,

"Thank you, Ricardo. It's great to see such non-touristy sights. So, where are we going?"

"I thought I would take you to my favorite restaurant. Only the locals know about it."

The car pulled up to a Spanish-style building: red tiled roof, stucco walls, and rounded arches. A valet ran out and opened the car doors. Ricardo slipped his hand under her elbow and guided her up the uneven, stony steps. Sarah enjoyed the old-fashioned touch from a true gentleman.

Sarah noticed a brass plaque by the door, which displayed the name *La Gaviota, desde 1987* in an elegant font. "Impressive," Sarah remarked, "Maintaining a restaurant for that duration is no small feat."

Indeed," Ricardo replied, "It's a testament to the enduring quality and appeal of the place. If only these walls could talk."

Inside a symphony of enticing aromas enveloped Sarah; she knew she was in for a culinary experience beyond the ordinary. There wasn't an empty chair in the whole place, but the moment they entered, the maître d' approached them and smiled. He said a few words in Spanish, then Ricardo introduced Sarah.

"I do apologize, *señorita*. I didn't realize that you did not speak Spanish."

"I do speak a little and hope to learn a lot more while I'm here."

The maître d' led them through the crowded salon, past the inner courtyard, to a secluded table at the far end of a wide balcony. Sarah admired the interior, a seamless blend of modern elegance and authentic Mexican charm. Rich, earthy tones of wood and stone were enhanced by vibrant splashes of color, creating a visually inviting space. She listened to the soft, ambient music playing in the background, which added to the serene atmosphere. She took notice of the impeccably dressed staff moving gracefully among the tables, expertly balancing sizable, weighty trays above their heads.

She looked over at the bar, which displayed an array of premium Tequilas and Mezcal, and Sarah observed with fascination as the bartender expertly mixed cocktails, orchestrating each movement that resembled a dance. It reminded her a time when she tended bars a few years back,

She leaned over the railing to admire the view and breathe in the salt air. The bay sprawled from one end of the island to the other. Lights flickered from the fishing boats like a Christmas tree. Small villas dotted the coastline. She sat down, and the waiter arrived. "Beautiful, isn't it?"

"Incredible," replied Sarah.

"I'm glad you like it," said Ricardo. "Would you like a drink?"

Sarah ordered a Brandy Alexander, her favorite cocktail, and Ricardo ordered Scotch. The aroma wafting from the passing dishes intensified Sarah's hunger. Their drinks arrived, and the waiter took their order. During their conversation, Ricardo told her that he had been born in Mexico City, educated in England, and owned a business in America. He had returned to Mexico due to family business which was keeping him longer than expected.

Their meal began with hearts of palm in a cream sauce, followed by red snapper and vegetables cooked just how she liked them, steamed and crunchy. Ricardo told her how much more beautiful the town looked when this restaurant was first built.

"Tourists were supposed to boost the economy, but instead, crime increased and harmed the tourist trade for a couple of years," he said, "but slowly the new mayor was making incredible improvements, raising wages for local police who were trying to keep crime to a minimum, especially the drug-related crime."

"Wow! A politician who is actually doing something for the good of the people. I can't stand drugs," said Sarah, "they bring so much grief to all concerned. I have had some experience with bad choices of roommates."

Ricardo's brow furrowed.

"What's wrong Ricardo, you look a little sad?"

"I'm sorry. It's just that a friend of mine was killed in crossfire from a drug cartel dispute, and then a few months, ago my brother was killed. Wrong place at the wrong time."

"Oh, my God! I'm so sorry."

"I shouldn't have brought it up," said Ricardo. "It's okay. Would you like more wine?"

He filled both their glasses and Sarah took a large sip. "Do you miss living here?" said Sarah.

"Well, I am lucky to have enough money and time to come back as often as I like. It keeps my mother happy too."

She was tempted to ask more about his family but decided this was not the right time. After they finished off a bottle of Beaujolais, Sarah leaned back in her chair as she listened to one of Ricardo's amusing stories of his time in university in England.

"A few weeks into the semester, I had fully embraced the British culture, but still loved to throw in a bit of my Mexican flair. One day, my friends decided to have a traditional British tea party. So, I wanted to contribute, and offered to make guacamole. My friends were skeptical and laughed but agreed. I showed up to the tea party with a massive bowl of guacamole and a bag of tortilla chips."

Sarah burst out laughing, "Such sacrilege," she said.

Ricardo continued, "They sipped their tea and nibbled on cucumber sandwiches, then hesitantly tried the guacamole. To their surprise, they loved it! Soon, the guacamole was the star of the tea party, and my blend of British and Mexican traditions became a hit for the rest of the semester."

" I do love guacamole, but not when drinking tea," said Sarah.

When the dessert tray arrived, she chose jericalla, the closest she could get to a crème brulee. "This is the best part of the meal," she said, licking the last bite of dessert from the spoon. "It was a wonderful meal, but I think I ate a little too much."

"Let me order you a liqueur to help your digestion."

"Just a small one, please," she said.

"Okay, and wouldn't you like to smoke?"

"No, I gave it up again."

"Good, it's a terrible habit."

"Are you trying to get me drunk?" she asked, a few minutes later as she stared at the huge shot of port.

"Never. We'll take a walk, and you'll feel invigorated."

As they walked on the sandy hillside in a comfortable silence, she pondered his words at dinner. He was intriguing. He said he came here on family business but never mentioned a wife or children, but she still wasn't prepared for a new relationship, as John still lingered in her thoughts. She breathed in the cool night air and admired the twinkling bright stars in the gray-blue sky. It was so peaceful.

"You should see this view in the daylight. There are several different beaches, so you can have a different one to yourself every day with no tourists," said Ricardo.

They strolled slowly until midnight, finally making their way back to the car. Sarah did not want the evening to end. She was happy when he drove her back to the hotel at a leisurely pace. He stopped the car in front of the hotel. "Are you busy tomorrow?"

"Actually, I have a dinner date. I'm sorry."

"It's okay. I just don't want you to feel alone. If you need help or companionship, just call me." He handed her his business card. "How about dinner the day after tomorrow? I'll pick you up at three p.m. so I can show you some sights before we eat."

Before she could reply, he kissed her lightly on the cheek. She nodded her head and watched him lower himself into his car and drive off, leaving her standing in a daze. It had appeared she had agreed to spend most of the day with him.

The valet opened the door of the hotel, and she floated through, savoring the sensation of Ricardo's lips against her cheek. The sound of Charles' voice jolted her from her dreamlike state. "Told you they were all Romeos here."

"Really, Charles, you're a little early, aren't you? Dinner isn't until tomorrow!"

Lifting the glass in his hand, he said, "Don't be late."

Sarah walked through the lobby and upstairs to her room. She slammed the door. She hoped he didn't make a habit of sounding jealous and saying dumb things.

Sitting in a hot bath, bubbles flowing freely, she relaxed and recapped her wonderful evening with Ricardo. She wondered whether she should cancel her dinner with Charles tomorrow, but decided against it as it would be Christmas Eve. Normally, she didn't celebrate the holidays, however, here in Mexico she was feeling a little more sociable. She crawled under the clean, cool sheets and fell into a deep slumber.

6

As Sarah attempted her yoga practice on the plush carpet, she found herself slipping into child's pose, her mind drifting back to her youth. Yoga and Zumba had become integral parts of her life, which had been crucial during her years of dance lessons. She had once danced for a small company, and even now, although she would never dance professionally again, she continued to enjoy her current dance classes. In addition, she had recently taken up salsa classes, hoping to put her new skills to use during her trip to Mexico. These activities not only kept her in shape but also allowed her to indulge her passion for dance and movement.

Yoga just wasn't in the cards, so she made her way down to the restaurant. While eating a large salad, she observed the usual combination of ingredients with the addition of watermelon. The contrast between the familiar and the unexpected reminded her of the differences between Charles and Ricardo. Charles came across as charming, handsome, and open, but Sarah couldn't tolerate jealousy, even in a friendship, and casual sex just wasn't in her DNA. Ricardo, with his impulsiveness and carefree joie de vivre, mixed with an air of mystery, treated her like a younger sister. As Sarah contemplated her upcoming dinner with Charles that evening, she knew deep down that once she returned home, she would likely never see either of them again.

She made a conscious decision to stop worrying about everything and focus on having fun during her time in Mexico. With this mindset, she looked forward to whatever adventures and experiences lay ahead.

The sun was shining, and there was a slight breeze, so she strolled barefoot from one end of the beach to the other. The sound of the waves rolling onto the shore had a calming effect on her as the salty water swirled around her feet. The sea was a bluish green, and she watched the children laugh and play with the large pieces of seaweed brought in with the tide.

It was a peaceful walk. She returned to her hotel room to relax, cool off, and read her novel.

'The knock on the door startled her. She wasn't expecting anyone. "Who is it?" she asked. A muffled voice with a heavy accent replied, "Room service."

"Sorry, you have the wrong room." The squeaky wheels of the food trolley moved into the distance, but the heavy footsteps became louder. Then they stopped. She listened and heard nothing, so moved silently towards the door. The handle turned.

"Who's there?" she shouted. Feeling a panic sweep over her, she moved closer to the door, and just as it swung open....'

Sarah inserted the bookmark and put down her novel. It was time to get ready, so she headed for the shower. Finally, some hot water, which steamed up the bathroom to turn it into her own personal sauna. Sarah dressed leisurely to make sure everything was perfect. Looking in the mirror, she admired the long black dress. The thigh-length split at the side showed off one long leg. The tan helped cover the small scars, alleviating her self-consciousness. She fastened the simple gold chain around her neck and set off confidently, looking forward to the evening ahead of her.

She was only five minutes late meeting Charles. Sarah had to admit he looked stunning, standing there by the fountain, dressed in white trousers and a navy jacket. She thought that if he had purposely arranged the meeting place for effect, it worked. The sophisticated, stylish way he dressed only added to his irresistible charm.

"You look mahvellous, darling," he said.

"You don't look so bad yourself," she said laughing at his exaggerated accent.

"Let's go. I found this spiffy restaurant. You'll love it."

Sarah and Charles climbed into a waiting taxi. The night sky was clear, adorned with bright, twinkling stars that seemed to shine just for her. Any doubts she had about this evening with Charles quickly dissipated as if the night breeze had whisked them away.

They drove past the usual hangouts, where tourists eagerly sampled new restaurants and people lined up to be seen at trendy nightclubs. This wasn't Sarah's scene; she preferred the ambiance of quiet jazz clubs.

As they approached the restaurant La Gaviota, Sarah's recognition stirred a mix of emotions. It was the same place she had dined with Ricardo, and a flutter of butterflies danced in her stomach. The coincidence felt eerie, though she reminded herself that five-star restaurants were not on every corner in this picturesque location. Charles clearly appreciated the finer things in life, so must have done his research. The taxi pulled up outside the restaurant, and they made their way inside. Sarah silently hoped that the waitstaff were either too preoccupied to recognize her or that this was a different crew from the previous night shift.

Charles, grinning broadly, noted Sarah's reaction. "I know, it's beautiful, but you don't have to look so dumbfounded."

"I suddenly have a feeling of déjà vu," she confessed.

"Usually, it's only frequented by the locals, but I have a knack for finding exotic places," he said modestly as they took their seats.

To Sarah's relief, they were seated at a table far away from the one she had sat at only yesterday. Why should she feel guilty? Should she mention her previous visit? No! Why? It would burst Charles' light-hearted mood. It's not like she was dating either of them.

As the waiter handed Sarah a menu, she felt a slight blush creeping up her cheeks, a momentary reminder of the time she had spent with Ricardo. However, with Charles by her side now, she was determined to savor the evening and make the most of it. Hiding behind the menu, she composed herself. She relaxed into the plush leather chair, took a deep breath, lowered the menu, and smiled warmly. Charles beamed back at her then continued to peruse the menu, and Sarah put thoughts of Ricardo to the back of her mind.

"Are you ready to order?" he said.

"Yes, I'm going to have the Santa Lucia Salad and the fish of the day."

"Good choice. I'll order the wine. Did you know Mexico produces some wonderful wines?"

"No, I have read about ruins and missions but not wine." Sarah listened with interest and leaned forward slightly; her gaze fixed intently on him as he spoke. A small smile tugged at the corners of her lips; her eyebrows raised in subtle admiration. The way his words painted a vivid picture of the vineyards and their history left her pleasantly surprised and genuinely impressed. He rounded off the conversation.

"My favorite is Casa Madero, which offers a rich bouquet of ripe berries, plum, and a hint of spice. It is just well-balanced with a smooth lingering finish."

Charles then placed their order in Spanish. Despite his less-than-perfect language skills, Sarah appreciated the effort he made to engage with the local culture and language. They chatted effortlessly.

"So, how long are you staying in Mexico?" asked Sarah.

"Not sure. I haven't had a holiday in so long. What about you?"

"I planned on two weeks," she said.

"How come you ended up in the States?"

"My father was American and I had always wanted to visit. I went to Los Angeles and liked it so much, I stayed."

"That sounded like past tense. Are your parents not alive?"

Sarah had developed the habit of sharing only a brief version of her life story with people she didn't know well, including her time with her foster parents.

"Not sure. I was brought up by foster parents. Do you see your parents often," said Sarah quickly changing the subject.

"Yes, I am lucky. They are great people. I always wish I had a brother though."

Although Sarah felt that he was also reluctant to talk about himself, she felt a sense of relief that the conversation had shifted, allowing her to focus on the meal in front of her.

The food was again delicious, and Charles' choice of wine was perfect. As the waiter cleared the dishes, Charles asked Sarah if she would like dessert.

Sarah laughed, "No, I have a few extra unwanted pounds."

"I was looking forward to their special."

"Go ahead," said Sarah.

"Can't. It's for two."

The waiter strolled to their table with the dessert cart, and Sarah's eyes widened.

Sarah laughed, "You've convinced me. I am a bit of a chocoholic."

The waiter brought a large piece of chocolate fudge cake covered in whipped cream, along with two spoons, and they dipped into the luscious chocolate. After three or four spoonfuls, their giggles turned to a provocative silence. Their eyes met. They slowly leaned closer to each other and wiped off whipped cream from each other's lips with their fingertips. The dessert was gone, yet their faces stayed close. Sarah felt the attraction but pulled away before a kiss would ensue. She leaned back.

"Oh, that was yummy." Her statement and posture broke the sexual tension. "I feel so guilty; I know I ate some of your share."

Charles took her hand gently in his. "How about a walk on the beach?"

"Maybe another time," said Sarah remembering her time with Ricardo.

"Well, we should have some kind of exercise," he said with a wicked smile.

She stroked his hand slowly; it was soft and well-manicured. She looked straight at him and said in a soft voice, "Yes, we should. Let's go—" she deliberately paused, before adding, "dancing."

Laughing, Charles stood up, pulled back her chair, and then held her hand on the way to the exit as the doorman hailed them a taxi.

In the taxi back, they stayed silent. Sarah leaned against Charles' shoulder as he massaged her fingers. She felt the magic. One part of her wanted to be cautious and pull away from his grasp, as she would soon be back in Los Angeles, working her ten-to-twelve-hour days. On the other hand, she longed for wild abandon to consume her with the passion she hadn't felt since John had left her.

As they entered Viva! nightclub, Sarah's senses were assaulted by the vibrant chaos of the place. The nightclub was large, illuminated only by flashing and spinning lights, and the noise was deafening. Sarah wondered how long she could handle the sensory overload.

"I hope there is somewhere less noisy," she said.

"What did you say?" shouted Charles.

"It's too noisy to talk," she shouted back.

"Follow me—it's too noisy to talk," he said. He grabbed her hand, and they entered a room where a four-piece band were playing. People were gently tapping their feet to the beat of the music while others were peacefully sipping their cocktails. In one corner, a couple was locked in a passionate kiss. Sarah followed Charles to a table.

He leaned in and kissed her on the cheek before asking what she would like to drink. Sarah was grateful for the dim, subtle lighting in the room as she felt herself blushing under his affectionate gesture. Someone yelled, "Feliz Navidad!"

Everyone was in good spirits and drinking plenty of them too. Christmas Eve in Mexico was more like New Year's Eve—one big party. The drinks arrived, but before she could take a sip, the band started playing a lively salsa tune. The trumpet blared loudly, and the lead singer swayed his hips to the infectious rhythm. Charles pulled her onto her feet saying, "You ready for this?"

With a playful tone, she told Charles, "If you can do this, then I'm yours forever." she answered, deciding to put her dance lessons to the test.

Sarah loved dancing but found most men she met couldn't keep up with her. However, she and Charles managed to look as if they had danced together before, and Charles was clearly having a great time.

"You're dancing superbly this evening," she complimented him.

"You too, Ginger."

The music stopped. "Let's sit!" said Sarah, her breath uneven.

"Just one more," said Charles.

As the music shifted to a slow and sensual rhythm, Sarah didn't have the energy to resist. She rested her head on Charles' shoulder, and they both swayed to the music. Charles held her close, and she felt his heart pounding rapidly. Sarah nestled into him, burying her face in the curve of his neck, and he responded by gently kissing the top of her head. Sarah's face flushed with emotion as they swayed together, lost in the music and each other's presence. Sarah and Charles were so engrossed in their slow dance that they didn't notice when the music came to an end. As the last notes faded away, they suddenly became aware of their solitude on the empty dance floor. Sarah's eyes widened slightly, and she exchanged a sheepish smile with Charles.

She pulled away. "I need a drink!"

They sat down but were abruptly interrupted by the arrival of Harry Whelan and his friends, including a striking blonde woman. Trying to hide her irritation, Sarah grabbed her drink, slurping a little too loudly. Sarah couldn't help but feel curious and a little jealous as the woman positioned herself between Charles and Harry and then kissed Charles on the cheek.

"I didn't expect you until tomorrow, Sylvia," Charles said.

"Obviously," she said, staring at Sarah.

Her presence was striking, from her designer outfit to her dazzling smile. Her jewelry made Sarah's Cartier ring look like a trinket from Walmart.

"Sarah, I'd like you to meet Sylvia, er, an old friend of mine."

"Careful with the old," she purred, "Come on darling, I feel like dancing," and whisked him onto the dance floor.

As Sarah observed Charles and Sylvia's interactions, a mix of emotions swirled within her. She couldn't help but wonder about the nature of their relationship. Was Sylvia an ex-girlfriend? The ease with which they conversed and their apparent comfort with each other raised questions in Sarah's mind. She felt a pang of jealousy, despite having just met Charles.

The music changed to a slow beat and Charles and Sylvia moved close, a little too close for Sarah's comfort, but then as she watched, she thought they were having more of a serious conversation then a romantic one. She noticed Harry was watching them too.

"Would you like to dance darling?" asked Harry.

"I'm sorry, I have to go to the ladies room." replied Sarah.

While she was washing her hands, she looked at her reflection: she looked exhausted. Sensing someone behind her, she turned to see a voluptuous Mexican girl with eyes the color of emeralds.

"Hello," said Sarah. The girl didn't reply, so she repeated it in Spanish.

41

"I speak very well English," the girl told her. "Your name is Sarah, is it not?"

"Who are you? How do you know my name?"

She didn't answer but moved closer to Sarah and whispered, "Stay away from Ricardo. He's dangerous, but more important, he belongs to me." With that, she stormed out.

Sarah wasn't sure how to react. Was this young woman dangerous, or just being melodramatic?

When Sarah arrived back at the table, Charles and Sylvia were sitting close together, holding hands, so she decided she'd had enough excitement for one night.

"Charles, I think I'll be going. I feel a little tired."

"Wait. I'll walk you back to the hotel." He walked her towards the door when Sarah turned to face him.

"How dare you! You wine and dine me, bring me to a romantic setting and then flirt with another woman." she whispered angrily.

"I can explain. I ..."

Sarah held up her hand, "Don't bother. I saw the way she looked at you. And I am quite capable of walking back to my hotel alone." She turned and hurriedly walked out the door with Charles staring after her.

"Darling," said Sylvia, "Let her go. Can't you see she wants to be alone?"

Sarah walked back to the hotel. Instead of the ocean's salty air, tonight the pungent smell of piled-up trash took precedence. It would remain there until after Christmas now. She crossed the square to the hotel and past the crowded bar to the elevator. She thought about Charles and Sylvia, and the way Harry sat watching them – something didn't sit right. Charles's attentive behavior had changed from the moment

Sylvia arrived. They were intimate, but not like lovers.

She wished she had gotten Sylvia's last name so she could Google her. Right now, her head was fuzzy. All she wanted to do was sleep. The combination of wine and dancing had taken its toll. As her tired body quickly drifted off into slumber, she hoped the next day would bring more clarity to the situation.

7

As the fiery, orange sun rose above the mountains, Sarah moved further under the shade of the blue-and-white umbrella that jutted out of the wrought iron table. She sipped on her iced coffee, then closed her eyes, lifting her head up to the sun. The Mexican influence brought back pleasant memories of experiences she had encountered in Italy and Spain. She often thought about returning to Europe. Maybe the south of France or a Greek island. She was tired of the big cities, especially Los Angeles, but that's where her livelihood was for the moment.

Sarah beckoned the waiter for a hot coffee this time. He delivered it with a smile. The strong aroma filled her nostrils as she mindlessly stirred the coffee. She reflected how, in only a couple of days, she had gained the attention of two men. But who was the girl in the nightclub bathroom who talked about Ricardo, and what was the relationship between Charles and Sylvia? She kept telling herself not to worry as nothing was going to happen with either of them. She sipped her coffee and contemplated her options, then walked across the road and rented a moped. She picked up some snacks and a bottle of water and rode off to explore the countryside. She had to find a hotel where she could stay for the rest of her vacation as the present one was booked through the end of the month. She had been lucky to get those days over Christmas due to someone canceling their reservation last minute.

Her riding skills improved after a few precarious moments. The roads were narrow and badly in need of repair, which gave her little room to dodge other inexperienced tourists maneuvering their rental cars. She hoped to find a quiet little hotel in Santa Maria, a quaint town only four miles away. It had more family-run inns and seaside cafes, and only a handful of deluxe properties. She stopped at several, but no rooms were available.

Hot, tired, and frustrated, she turned to go back when she came across a small hotel on the outskirts of the town. The rooms were small and bare but extremely clean. The sheets were paper thin, and the towels felt a little rough as they probably had been dried outside under the hot sun. Satisfied, she reserved a room for five nights with a small deposit.

As she looked around, she passed a cage with a parrot—its feathers a vivid green with patches of red. It spoke to her, but she couldn't understand the *bird Spanish*. Then, she laughed at its wolf whistle. The view from the inn was breathtaking. Sarah gazed out at the vast expanse of the bay, the crystal-clear waters shimmering in the sunlight. She marveled at the natural beauty of the area, the tranquility of the scene soothing her soul. She looked nervously at a couple of cockerels precariously perched on a tree. Could these creatures fly? If not, one false move, and they would be smashed to pieces on the impact of the fall into the ravine twenty feet below.

The owners, Maria and Jose, were Mexican Indians. They managed the place and were extremely friendly. Although they didn't speak much English, they understood Sarah's schoolbook Spanish. Sarah immediately fell in love with their daughter Daria, who stood there and peeked out from behind her mother, who said something to her in Spanish. Daria slowly approached Sarah, allowing her curiosity to overcome her shyness. She was in dire need of a bath. Her hair was dusty and tangled, her eyes big and brown, and her smile enchanting. Sarah handed her some candy, then reluctantly dragged herself away. Children always seemed to gravitate toward her. She had the same effect on cats. This brief encounter solidified Sarah's resolve to pursue becoming a foster mother. It also planted the seed for her future aspirations to adopt a child, regardless of her marital status.

Sarah traveled down a deserted road and followed some old road signs. They led her to the crumbling ruins of a fortress. She secured the moped, grabbed her backpack, and sauntered to the gate. A placard with tourist information hung above the entrance.

'Built in 1553 by Zapotec Indians, this fortress originally sprawled over 25 miles, with palaces, temples, and sports fields'.

Sarah sat for a few moments, in awe of the rich history of this country. She imagined the events that possibly had unfolded here, the stories of ancient civilizations, and the battles fought to protect this strategic vantage point.

She followed a pathway, passed a few tourists, and took some pictures of the fortress before heading home. She arrived back at her hotel exhausted but exhilarated. She enjoyed traveling alone sometimes.

As she packed her case to prepare for the move, the phone rang. It was Charles.

"Hi," she said without enthusiasm.

"Where have you been all morning?" he asked. "I looked for you everywhere."

"Really?" she replied. "I thought you and Sylvia would be sunning yourselves on some romantic beach."

"Ha!" he jested. "Do I detect a little green monster?"

Sarah resented his attitude. "Actually, I visited the old fortress in the next town. I do enjoy being alone sometimes."

"Let's have a late lunch in half an hour. I'll meet you downstairs."

She was about to say no, but she was hungry. "Okay, I'll see you then."

During lunch, he explained that Sylvia was an old friend of the family and was visiting friends in Mexico City. She knew that some of the old gang were back here and wanted to catch up with all the news. "There is absolutely no love interest, I assure you."

"It didn't look that way last night."

Charles just smiled and said, "She's very flirtatious, as well as attractive—"

Sarah punched him in the arm.

"—and under that tough exterior, she really is quite sensitive," he added.

"Oh, please. From what I saw, I don't believe you."

"But I'm telling you the truth."

Sarah couldn't believe that she felt jealous. Or was it that she didn't trust him after her situation with John? "Charles, you embarrassed me. We were having a great time, and then she arrived, and you totally ignored me. I had to walk back to my hotel alone."

"Hey, I did offer to accompany you."

"Right. But you and Sylvia looked so cozy."

"You mean, you and I could have had a lovely night of lovemaking?"

"Well, my dear, you will never know, will you? Let's eat. I'm starving."

They ate pita bread sandwiches and drank several glasses of iced tea.

"So, did you decide on how long you will be in Mexico?" asked Sarah.

"Just until the day after New Year. Then I need to visit Washington on a business trip and then back to London. Why? Are you planning to come visit me?"

Sarah laughed uncomfortably.

"What's wrong? Don't you believe in long-distance relationships?"

Sarah looked at him with a crooked smile. "I think long-distance relationships can work for a short while. No one wants to make a wrong decision when considering such a big move. But honestly, if I decide to move anywhere, it will be somewhere in Europe."

Charles took hold of Sarah's hand. "We're going to get married one day."

Sarah was taken aback and hoped he was joking, but with her quick wit, she hastily replied, "God, you haven't seen me naked yet."

He laughed, "But I have seen your soul through your eyes."

Totally embarrassed, she quipped, "Dream on. By the way, what is it exactly that you do for a living?"

"I'm a spy."

Sarah froze remembering that John used to say the same thing. "Geez, I'm supposed to be the joker."

Charles leaned back in his chair, a thoughtful expression on his face. "If you must know, I'm involved in international trade and business consulting. It's a rather broad field, but let's just say I help companies expand their horizons, navigate foreign markets, and, sometimes, I dabble in a bit of investment management."

Sarah raised an eyebrow. "Sounds intriguing."

Charles chuckled. "I suppose you could say that. It allows me to travel quite a bit, which I enjoy."

Sarah nodded, feeling a mixture of curiosity and caution. "Okay, enough chatter, let's go to the beach."

"Okay! I'll see you in ten minutes," said Charles.

Sarah reached the beach five minutes late.

"A true lady," joked Charles, "always keep a gentleman waiting."

"At least I recognized you to be a gentleman."

"Is your Latin lover a gentleman?"

"Look, if you are going to act jealous and be rude, then I'll leave you to check out the other women on the beach. There's a real cute blonde over there in the water trying not to get her hair wet."

Charles grabbed her hand and pulled her onto the sand. "You don't get away that easily."

They laughed as Sarah threw her towel at him. She slipped off her dress, revealing a modest bikini complimenting her trim figure. She glanced at Charles, whose eyes rested on her small but firm breasts and slender long legs. As their eyes met, he turned away.

They lay back in the sun for a while, and then Charles asked, "Did you visit the beach much when you were growing up in England?"

"Yes. Those tides came in so quickly, we had to scramble to stop our towels and belongings getting wet. One minute we were sunning, next almost swimming. I also remember giggling at the old men sitting around in the striped deck chairs with the knotted hankies on their heads."

"So, when you lived in London, did you ever visit Brighton and go on the pier?" said Charles.

"Oh, yes. I don't know why I'm not fat with all those cakes and biscuits we demolished at the local tea shops."

Charles tapped his tummy. "Yup."

They chatted easily for an hour. Sarah glanced down at her red skin and pushed back a head of sweaty hair. "I think that's enough sun for me," she said as she gathered up her clothes.

"I have a business meeting tonight, or I would offer you dinner."

"Really? I thought you were on vacation."

"I am," replied Charles, "but always looking for ways to make money."

"It's okay. I have a dinner date anyway."

Charles glanced at her but said nothing. They walked back to the hotel. Before they parted, Charles planted a gentle kiss on her cheek. Then his mouth searched for hers. The kiss grew passionate and demanding and took Sarah by surprise. She pulled away gently and blushed.

"Sorry," said Charles, "just couldn't help myself."

Sarah smiled and licked her lips. I'm not sorry, she thought. This guy can kiss. I should just grab him and take him to my room.

They agreed to meet the next day and visit another local attraction. Sarah needed a nap, so she went straight to her room, curled up on the bed, and fell into a peaceful sleep until the phone rang. It was Ricardo.

"You have the knack of awakening me from my dreams," she teased.

"I'm sorry. I also have to say I'm sorry that I must break our dinner engagement tonight, but I would like to make it up to you. Tomorrow evening. Same time, same place?"

Sarah truly meant it when she said it was okay. She was able to enjoy her solitary afternoon by the pool, basking in the warm sun and relishing the feeling of tranquility that enveloped her. She sipped on a refreshing drink, occasionally taking bites of her snack.

'*She looked over to the other side of the pool and saw a short, stocky man dressed in slacks and shirt, staring at her. He looked totally out of place. He turned away a little too quickly. She thought he looked familiar but couldn't think from where. He picked up his sunglasses and walked toward the hotel. Oh, my God, was that a gun she saw as his shirt blew in the breeze? Then she remembered where she had seen him—in the restaurant, two days ago*'.

"Would you like another drink, ma'am?" asked the waiter.

"Just the bill, please," she replied as she closed her book.

Back in her hotel room, she wrote some postcards and then slowly drifted off to sleep much earlier than intended.

Manuel Vittorio de Costa sat poolside at his villa, engrossed in conversation on his mobile phone. The fragrance of vibrant red bougainvillea wafted in the air. As he ended the call, Carmen entered. "You wanted to see me, *Don* Manuel?" she asked, using his official name while discreetly checking to ensure none of his men were nearby. Despite only being his niece, he preferred to be called 'Papa'—but only when they were alone.

He gazed at her, struck by her youth and vulnerability. Her long black hair shimmered in the sunlight, and her emerald-green eyes seemed to pierce right through him.

Manuel hoped that once Ricardo had concluded his business

in the area, he would take Carmen with him to America. After Carmen's parents passed away, Manuel and his second wife, Ana, raised her as their own daughter. They had briefly lived in America, but since Manuel's return to Mexico, Ana had found every excuse to stay in the United States. While no one was certain why Manuel had married Ana, besides her obvious beauty, it was clear that she valued money and freedom more than a traditional family life. Manuel moved back to Mexico as he saw a significant opportunity to amass wealth there, and he intended to seize it. However, he wanted more for Carmen. He wanted her to have an education, attend college, meet honest young men, and experience a normal life.

"Yes, Cara, please sit down," he said, gesturing to a chair.

Carmen sat across from him and offered her charming smile. Manuel knew that she could get almost anything she wanted from him, but this time, Manuel's expression remained stern. Carmen looked uncomfortable as she fidgeted with the ring that had once belonged to her mother.

"Jose told me he found you at the old stables yesterday. I've told you they're off-limits. What were you doing there?" Manuel asked, his tone serious.

Carmen replied, "I was just checking on the horses; I thought I would take a ride today."

Manuel breathed a sigh of relief, realizing that Carmen remained unaware of his main business. He always told her that he exported Tequila, which was true, but that alone couldn't support his extravagant lifestyle. As he chatted with her, he believed that she knew nothing about the drugs that were missing. Now, he had to find out who had taken them.

"You have plans to ride alone today?" Manuel inquired.

"*Si*, Papa, don't worry about me," Carmen replied. The

furrowed lines on her forehead smoothed out, and a gentle smile graced her lips as if the troubles that had been haunting her had melted away. She leaned in and kissed his cheek, but before turning to leave, she hesitated.

"Papa, I wasn't sure if I should mention this."

Manuel looked up. The corners of his mouth, which usually carried a casual demeanor, now down turned slightly, accompanied by a delicate frown. "You know you can tell me anything."

Carmen pulled out her phone and showed Manuel a photo.

"Who is this?"

"I don't know. I saw her hanging around the stables the other evening."

"Are you sure?"

"*Si*, Papa. So, when I saw her at the La Viva Club, I discreetly took her photo."

"Okay, let me look into it."

Carmen left but returned five minutes later, this time with Ricardo by her side. They laughed heartily together, and Manuel watched with a smile.

"*Buenos días*, Ricardo. Carmen, please excuse us. On your way out, kindly ask *Senora* Guevara to bring us some coffee."

Carmen pouted her lips and frowned as she reluctantly left the room. She stole a quick glance at Ricardo, but both he and Manuel were already engrossed in their discussion. She went to the kitchen, where *Senora* Guevara was already setting up a tray for coffee. She kissed the older woman on the cheek and said, "I'm so glad you're here, *senora.* I get tired of being the only woman."

Senora Guevara chuckled and replied, "*Vamos.*" The *senora* held a special affection for Carmen since she herself had no children or husband, yet she found contentment in her life. She had worked faithfully for *Don* Manuel for the past ten years, and he always treated her well. She sent most of her earnings to her ailing mother, whom she cared deeply for. *Senora* Guevara placed the tray on the ornate coffee table, greeted Ricardo, whom she genuinely admired, and then left the room, allowing their conversation to continue.

Sarah awoke to a beam of sunlight sparkling with suspended dust particles, shining through the window across the room. She felt refreshed and full of expectancy and opened the patio window to reveal a radiant blue sky. The warmth of the sunshine with just a hint of a gentle breeze filled the room. This was her last day in this hotel.

She dressed, then hurriedly ate breakfast before meeting Charles. They drove to Santa Maria, and Sarah pointed out her new hotel.

"Nice place—a little primitive," remarked Charles.

"Don't be such a snob!"

The rented car was comfortable, a far cry from her moped adventures. They traveled twenty-eight miles to the small pueblo of Tecoh to check out some Mayapan Yucatan ruins. Sarah, as a passenger, enjoyed the time to admire the scenery as Charles drove carefully through the narrow roads. As they walked around the tall, gray buildings, the place reminded Sarah of what she had read in history books.

"Do you know the history of this area, Charles?"

"No, I don't. Would you like to enlighten me?"

"Well, the historians called the Mayans 'the Greeks of the New World.' They discovered the use of zero before the Arabs, devised the most accurate calendar in existence, and built their settlements near 'cenotes,' which were water holes that linked up with underground channels."

"Oh, yes. The drug lords had a great time using them to transport their goods," interjected Charles.

Sarah rolled her eyes. "As I was saying, before I was rudely interrupted, one of the theories for their extinction was that the water just dried up, maybe a punishment from God for all those victims that were sacrificed to their gods."

They walked a little further, and Sarah finished her history lesson. "However, their architectural genius lives on in the stately pyramids, and the tombs and temples."

They rested on top of a jagged wall. "This here was part of a mansion that lined the whole boulevard. That was when Merida was known as the *Paris of the West.*"

"Very interesting. You are just a walking history book."

Only a few tourists and a couple of scrawny dogs were present, so they enjoyed the peaceful surroundings without a crowd. Like teenagers, they joked around. Sarah and Charles posed for selfies and snapped pictures of the ruins. Charles asked Sarah to sit on a rock and pose for the next shot. "Darn it!" said Charles.

"What?" asked Sarah.

"This bloke got in the way of my perfect photo. Let's take another."

In a secluded spot, they came to an archway covered with ivy and made their way through it, then up a steep hill, discovering new tropical vegetation and undergrowth neither of them recognized. Almost breathless, they reached the top and sat on a large rock, which overlooked a sandy bay called Los Gatos, a place that was only accessible by boat or by climbing rugged terrain. As they admired the view, Charles suggested they visit Los Gatos one day.

"Hopefully, we'll take the ferry," joked Sarah.

The view was breathtaking. They could see for miles. The sapphire-blue ocean was flat like an ice pond: no waves, only slight ripples. Occasionally, a bird would dive in and grab a fish in its beak. To the right, the more expensive resorts dotted the shoreline, and to the left was an old fishing village that hadn't changed in the last twenty years or so.

Sarah found solace in his company, relishing the moments spent together that provided a welcome distraction from the thoughts of John. His presence was a respite from the emotional complexities that lingered in her mind. As they engaged in conversation and shared laughter, Sarah felt very relaxed.

On the way back down, an uncomfortable feeling that someone was following them overtook her. Just then, Charles yelled at her. She heard a rumble and turned to see rocks flying down the hill, kicking up white dust. The next moment, she was flung to the side and landed face down in the dirt with Charles on top of her. The dust and rocks kept falling, narrowly missing them. Charles lay protecting her with his strong body warding off danger. When the dust finally settled, Charles stood up. His breathing was heavy as he stood close to Sarah.

Sarah's throat felt so dry she could hardly breathe. Charles helped her back to her feet. She steadied herself by holding onto his arm and felt his pulse racing. She looked at him and to relieve the tension, said, "Really, Charles, you don't have to go to such lengths to get my attention."

"Always the comic," he said.

"I always joke when I'm nervous." Sarah's life had been more adventurous than most, but she'd never experienced true danger like this.

They stood there in stunned amazement, surveying the chaos

from the fallen rocks. Sarah assured him she was not hurt. He took her hand and gently led her down the hill. She had to jump the last few feet and landed awkwardly in Charles' strong arms.

"Do you think that was an accident?" Sarah asked.

"Of course," he replied. "What else? We are the only ones around, and it is possible that voices can cause small avalanches."

"But... I thought I saw someone following us!"

"I think you're mistaken," he said as he wiped dust from her hair. "Let me take a few shots of it before we leave."

He released her from his arms, took some pictures, and once again held her hand. They walked silently a few feet and then stopped. Charles turned to her affectionately and said,

"You know, I like you a lot."

"Thank you. I like you too."

Their eyes locked. Charles leaned over and kissed her tenderly, and in that moment, a surge of intense emotions, blending both desire and longing. momentarily eclipsing the fear that had recently gripped her. As their lips met, she couldn't help but experience hidden emotions—was it genuine affection or merely the residual adrenaline from recent events? They looked at each other. Sarah had dirt in and around her mouth, and Charles was covered in dust, which made them break out into uncontrollable laughter.

Each became lost in their own thoughts as the journey home faded into silence. Sarah realized the next few days with Charles could be very enjoyable.

"Are you free for dinner, or have I lost out to that Mexican?"

"His name is Ricardo," she snapped.

"Sorry, I'm being rude."

"Look, he is just excited to show me around. I assure you

there is nothing romantic going on. I feel more like his little sister."

"Okay, if you say so," said Charles.

Lost in thought, Sarah pondered over her broken date with Ricardo. Or was it a date? He did say he didn't want her to feel alone in his country. However, when she saw Ricardo again, she needed to ask him about the young woman in the club. Now, she was asking herself how she really felt about Charles. Could this be just a holiday fling? But the real question was, was she over John?

Suddenly, Charles made a sharp left turn.

"My sense of direction is not great, but I'm sure you took a wrong turn," Sarah said.

Charles kept checking the rear-view mirror. "Yes, I er. . . maybe."

"What's wrong?" Sarah asked nervously.

"Hold on," he yelled as he took another sharp turn, tires screeching. He slowed down, turned to look out the back window, and continued at a steady pace.

"What's wrong, Charles?"

"Sorry, I thought we were being followed."

"Followed? I got that same feeling when we were at the ruins."

"It's not a feeling; I noticed the same car behind us since we left there."

"Why would anyone want to follow us?"

"I don't know," said Charles, breathing heavily.

When they arrived at the hotel, Charles asked her again if she was free for dinner.

"I'm having dinner with Ricardo, but I'll be through early. If you like, I can meet you in the club later."

"Fine," replied Charles.

She entered the hotel and asked the concierge if falling rocks at the ruins was a regular occurrence and, if so, why was there no sign posted to warn unsuspecting tourists.

He looked confused when she asked. "But, madam, that area you are referring to is off-limits and is boarded up."

"Well," she seethed, "someone just 'unboarded' it, and my friend and I were almost seriously injured."

"I am so sorry, madam. I will get someone to look into it."

Back in her room, she mulled over everything that had happened.

Had someone been following them? Was that really an accident? If not, why would anyone want to harm her or Charles? She certainly had no enemies that she could think of.

8

Back at the ranch as Ricardo leisurely savored his coffee, he thought about his meeting with *Don* Manuel. He made a conscious choice to stay clear of any mention regarding the drugs. He had a suspicion that Carmen may have taken or borrowed them. A fleeting thought crossed his mind—perhaps she had already returned them? However, he quickly dismissed the notion. His primary focus was on extracting information about the upcoming meeting from *Don* Manuel, and he didn't want to distract him with potentially delicate matters.

Fatigue settled in, evident in the weariness etched on Ricardo's face. He was doing a special favor for the DEA and hoped the last. His proficiency stemmed from specialized training in navigating the intricacies of drug-related investigations, and his linguistic skills and profound knowledge of the area made him the ideal candidate for the task at hand. The desire to return to the US and resume his retired life from the DEA weighed heavily on his mind. Noticing Charles's keen interest in Sarah, Ricardo subtly maneuvered himself to keep her close. It was a strategic move, a carefully crafted plan to ensure Charles would inadvertently reveal any valuable information to her. The bureau had informed Ricardo that an Englishman was involved with *Don* Manuel, making his task even more critical.

Sarah stared at her reflection in the mirror. She decided that she could live with the image staring back at her: Slender, but slightly scarred legs, a few extra pounds on the belly, and breasts, ... well, nothing's perfect. Her Ribkoff designer white top was paired with her black pants for tonight's festivities and, all in all, it was working... sexy and chic. Considering she had packed for a real vacation and not a dating spree, the limit of acceptable outfits was quickly running out. Maybe this was the perfect excuse for a shopping adventure. With a quick sashay, she moved away from the mirror and cruised around the room. The smooth swishing sound of her sleek black pants followed her every step. "I guess that's why they're called car wash pants," she giggled to herself. "I wonder why Americans call them pants and not trousers."

Arriving early for her dinner with Ricardo, she browsed the hotel gift shop, looking for suitable presents for friends back home. The only item she bought was a history book of the surrounding areas. In the lounge, she ordered a Tequila Sunrise and became absorbed in the book. Time was forgotten until she heard the bartender tell someone it was a little before eight. She paid her bill and rushed out to Cafe del Toro.

Sarah's heart raced as she watched the confrontation between Ricardo and the girl from the nightclub. It was an unexpected and uncomfortable sight. He was pointing a finger at her while his other hand, fist clenched, stayed by his side. The girl stood her ground, hands on hips, yelling back at him, then pushed him away and stormed off. Sarah stayed hidden in a doorway until the girl disappeared.

Sarah then slowly walked towards him. "You're late," he shouted.

Taken by surprise, she was about to yell back, but he took

her arm and sat her down a bit too roughly at the table. "I'm sorry," he said. "I have no right to be angry with you."

"Who was that girl?" Sarah asked.

"Her name is Carmen. She's the niece of a friend of mine."

Sarah listened to Ricardo's explanation, trying to make sense of the situation. It seemed like Carmen had some romantic interest in him, and this was causing friction. Sarah then told him about the incident in the club.

"I apologize," said Ricardo. "Since her parents died, her uncle looks after her, but she's left alone a lot and gets whatever she wants. She has a crush on me, and wants me to take her to America. Try to ignore her and anything she says; she has a vivid imagination." The waiter brought their coffee.

"Just to let you know, I will be moving to Santa Maria in a lovely *huespedas* called *Tres Marias*," said Sarah.

"Oh, a real Mexican family hotel," said Ricardo. "That's really sweet, but it's a bit far from town."

"I have to move out of my present hotel, and there was nothing else available," she said. "They are lovely people and have this gorgeous daughter."

"Actually, I have just the place for you. Finish your coffee, and we'll drive there now."

Two miles outside of town, they stopped in front of a beautiful, rustic villa. A large wrought iron gate sported two stone pillars on either side with ivy sprawling from top to bottom. The name above the gate said *Ranchero Castillo*. The driveway crunched as the car slowly made its way to the main entrance.

"This is incredible," she exclaimed as she got out of the car and approached the entrance. "How did you know about this place?"

Ricardo grinned. "I have my ways of finding hidden treasures.

I thought you might appreciate it."

A pleasant middle-aged Mexican lady wearing a crisp white apron greeted them at the door.

"*Buenos dias, Senor Ca—*"

"*Buenos dias, Senora* Magdelena," interrupted Ricardo.

"I have this young lady who needs a room for a few nights. Can you accommodate her?"

She looked at him, eyes wide and her mouth open, but no words came out. After a brief conversation in Spanish, the housekeeper smiled and asked Sarah to follow her up an elegant staircase that led to a large wooden door. As it swung open, Sarah's eyes swept the room. The tiled floor and colorful rugs exuded a sense of tradition and warmth, making her feel right at home. A patio door that looked out onto the old stables, together with the gentle sway of the ceiling fan, completed the picturesque scene. She took in a deep breath to catch the scent of the jasmine by the window.

She oohed, "This is beautiful."

"You stay here long time?" asked *Senora* Magdelena.

" *Si*, but, er... *quanto costa, senora? Esta es muy bonito.*"

"I know this *casa* beautiful... you ask the cost with *el senor*."

Sarah thanked her, turned to go downstairs, and came face to face with Ricardo.

"Ricardo, this place is wonderful, but I think it's too expensive."

"Don't worry." he said, smiling. "The owner is a friend of mine, and he owes me a favor."

"He owes you a favor, not me," she protested.

"*Es favor que usted me hace.* My favor is your favor, an old Mexican saying," he replied.

"You're crazy. I hardly know you; I just met you and..."

"If you feel guilty, you can help around the ranch."

"*Es favor que usted me hace.*"

"Your Spanish is improving," he said.

"Okay, I'll move here tomorrow, but I will pay the *huespedas* for the days I promised.

It's only fair."

"That's very noble of you. Now, let's do some sightseeing."

They drove to San Miguel, a haven for artists of every stripe and form. They wandered around and admired the colorful crafts, then ate at the elegant Casa de Sierra Nevada. Ricardo told Sarah that the owner had tastefully redesigned three handsome, colonial homes into an inn. Each house sheltered a courtyard of vibrant hibiscus and bougainvillea, while a maze of corridors, archways, and staircases led to eighteen spacious rooms. They sat in one that had its own fireplace with a splendid view of the town and ate dinner by candlelight. Sarah relaxed, looking at the man sitting across from her. She still didn't know too much about him, and when she tried to delve into his life, he always changed the conversation back to her, flattering her with compliments, which Sarah enjoyed immensely.

"Let me buy you dinner," said Sarah.

"Never," he replied adamantly.

"I insist, just to say thank you for what you've done."

"Okay," he relented. "Just this once."

After a short pause, she continued. "It's getting late. I'm sorry, but I have to go."

"I suppose you have a date with that young friend of yours?"

She laughed, "He's not much younger than you, and anyway, he did save my life."

Ricardo was immediately concerned. "What do you mean?"

She told him about the incident at the ruins.

"You tourists should read the signs," he said angrily.

"But I..." stammered Sarah.

"Never mind, let's go," he replied curtly as he escorted her out of the restaurant to his car. He looked distracted, not his usual self.

Silent and a little upset at his attitude, Sarah pulled her arm away and slid into the car seat.

"I'm sorry," he said. "I just worry about you, a young attractive lady on your own. This is a much different place than Los Angeles. Some places you just don't go to, especially if you are not from the area."

Sarah thought, What a lame argument. "Actually, it sounds just like LA."

"Okay," he laughed, "Of course!"

When they arrived at the club, Ricardo kissed her lightly on the cheek.

"Have fun, *hasta luego*."

Sarah nodded, then entered the club. It was a large place with an open-air terrace full of people dancing and drinking. The lights were low and the music incredibly loud.

I'll never find Charles in this swarm of people, she thought as she turned to leave.

"Hey baby, wanna drink?" Sarah was face to face with an obnoxious drunk.

"Sorry, I'm a teetotaler."

"Ah, a smart bitch," he slurred.

"Buzz off," she said calmly, trying not to attract attention.

He grabbed her arm. "You think you're too good for me, lady?"

She glared at him hard as the stench of stale alcohol lay on his breath. "Actually, intoxicated suitors aren't high on my list. Let go of my arm; you're hurting me."

"You had better do as the lady says," came Charles' voice, calmly but deadly, through the crowd.

The man reeled around and took a swing at Charles but missed. The return punch landed squarely on the man's jaw, knocking him to the floor. A group of onlookers applauded, snapping photos on their mobiles. It caught the attention of two doormen.

"Don't worry, sir. He's been asking for that all evening," said the taller of the two as they dragged him away.

"Well," said Sarah, "I guess you studied boxing in your public school."

"Boxing champ three years in a row," he boasted.

"Come on, Muhammad Ali, let me buy you a drink. I had better make it a double, as you saved my life twice today."

Charles laughed, "I thought you had changed your mind about coming."

"No, I owe you, remember?"

"So that's the only reason you came?"

"Now don't get an attitude. I came because I wanted to,"

Or did she? Would she rather be with Ricardo? She had enjoyed his company, but she did like Charles.

"Why is it I don't believe you?" he said.

They sat at a table while the waitress brought two drinks with paper umbrellas and fruit trimmings. Usually, Sarah drank wine, so after a couple of these Tequila cocktails, she felt lightheaded. It had been a strange day. Charles jumped up and took her by the hand. "Let's dance."

As before, they managed not to trip over each other's feet. They sat and had another drink. Sarah yawned and said,"I'm tired. I need to go. I have an early checkout as I'm moving."

Charles and Sarah arrived back at their hotel just after midnight. They chatted in the lobby, and Sarah felt the tension so kissed Charles on the cheek and said goodnight. Charles didn't let go of her hand and lingered. Sarah stood there motionless as she knew he expected more. As she turned towards the elevator, he reached for her, pulling her close. He kissed her gently on the lips. Her heart raced. Unsure, she pulled away before the kiss became more passionate. She felt guilty seeing the look of disappointment on his face.

"How about a nightcap in my room?" Charles suggested as he stroked her hand.

Sarah felt butterflies in her stomach, tempted to say yes. "I thought you were more original than that."

"What do you want me to say, come and spend the night with me?"

"At least that's more like the truth," she said. "I'm not ready for a brief affair at the moment."

Charles took her hand and said, "It's not like we would never see each other again."

"Oh, really." Sarah laughed. "I don't intend to commute to England every weekend."

"Well, I could always ask for a transfer," he replied.

"Let me take a rain check."

"Okay. If you change your mind, I'm in room 264."

9

Sarah trudged wearily up to her room. She opened the door and gasped. Bed covers were strewn on the floor, and the mattress was all askew. Drawers were half opened, and all her clothing was scattered on the floor. Nothing had gone untouched. The rug was pulled up, and even the trash can had been dumped. She called Charles immediately.

"I knew you would change your mind; I'll be right up," he said excitedly, then hung up before she could explain.

He must have run up the stairs, as he was breathing heavily when he knocked on Sarah's door. He walked in and was about to say something when he saw the chaos in the room. "Bloody hell! What happened in here?" said Charles, almost dropping his bottle of wine. He pushed past her and stepped over a pile of clothes then turned a full circle, his eyes sharp and sweeping. He strode over to the bathroom and kicked open the door to reveal another mess. "Sorry, I just want to make sure whoever did this isn't still hiding in here waiting for you. Is anything missing? What about your credit cards and cash?"

"Luckily, I had my credit card with me, and my passport is in the hotel safe." Sarah sucked in a deep, ragged breath. Her hand trembled as she swept back her hair from her pale face. "What on earth were they looking for?"

"I'll call hotel security."

"Thank you, Charles," said a distraught Sarah. "I'm grateful that you are here for me.

"Nothing like this has ever happened to me before, well, except when my bike was stolen. But to have someone in your personal space is creepy."

Security was quick to respond. They informed her that the local police were on their way and advised her to call the front desk to get a different room for the night. As the police took the report from Sarah, Charles hovered quietly in the background.

The police looked tired and disheveled as if they'd been dragged out of bed, which did not give Sarah much confidence in their capabilities.

After an hour, Charles and Sarah were alone. "Who could have done this?" said Charles.

"More importantly, why?" said Sarah. "I'm determined to get to the bottom of this."

"Would you feel safer staying with me?" asked Charles kindly.

Sarah looked at him, "Yeah, right!"

"No, I mean, you take the bed, and I'll sleep on the sofa."

"Thank you, Charles. You're very sweet, but I'll be fine. The hotel has arranged another room for me. I'll see you tomorrow."

"Let me at least walk you to your new room."

When they arrived, Sarah turned to give him a quick kiss on the cheek. She found her lips on his, and he kissed her gently. Her lips opened. The kiss deepened, quickly flooding them with passion as his tongue searched for hers. Sarah swiped the key card, and they stumbled into her room. Sarah's arms wound themselves around his neck, and his arms tightened around her, locking their bodies in an embrace that was rapidly becoming heated. His mouth claimed hers, deepening until she felt they were melting together. She felt the tension of the past couple of hours leaving her as his mouth began to trail searing kisses down her neck, and a moan escaped from her throat. With a low, triumphant laugh, he scooped her up, her arms still around his neck, and carried her over to the bed.

He was everything she had dreamed of—gentle and strong but soft and passionate, always concerned with her needs, taking his satisfaction from her pleasure. It was an incredible experience for her, and afterward she lay there with a sheen of sweat and lovemaking on her body, panting with still-felt passion. He lay next to her, smiling as he ran his fingers over her hips. She shivered from the touch, and he whispered, "More?"

Sarah turned and put her face into his neck, shaking her answer. He settled back, one arm holding her, and she felt him drop into a deep sleep almost instantly. She lay for a few minutes, her mind trying to make sense of what just happened. But exhaustion took over, and she relaxed, sated, and fell asleep curled up into his side like a kitten.

She woke up and stared at the digital clock. The green digits glared 4:00 AM. She was alone, so she assumed Charles had gone back to his own room.

10

At exactly eight o'clock, her phone rang and brought Sarah back to the living. Reluctantly, she picked up the phone and said, "Hello," in a raspy voice.

"Well, you sound like you must have had a great time last night," said Ricardo.

"Ricardo, could you call me back in a couple of hours? I'll explain later."

She replaced the receiver. Her head throbbed, so she grabbed a pillow to block her eyes from the daylight. She would need to have more sleep to get through the rest of the day. Ricardo wasn't to blame, as normally she would be up and about at this time. She was dozing off when the phone rang again.

"Merde," she mumbled.

"Hello, it's Harry. Is Charles there?"

"How dare you wake me up to ask such an impertinent question? Of course he isn't." She slammed down the phone, now wide awake. She climbed out of bed and as she passed by the mirror, she saw puffy, bloodshot eyes. She wanted to kill Harry. Too tired to go back to her old room and tackle the mess, she threw on some sweats and decided to call Charles. Why should he be allowed to sleep in? After all, it was his pal Harry who had finally gotten her out of bed.

She called him but got a 'do not disturb' signal. He's not getting off that easy, she thought. Maybe she could surprise him and have a quickie before breakfast. She showered quickly and dressed, grabbed her bag, and went down to his room. There was no answer when she knocked. A maid was happy to unlock his door for her, with the persuasive help from a ten-dollar bill.

"Charles," Sarah called as she stepped inside. There was no response. His bed was untouched. She tapped on the bathroom door. No response there either. She looked around and sighed. She liked Charles a lot, but this kind of mysterious behavior troubled her. As she made her way to the door, her purse caught on the metal bed frame and the contents spilled onto the floor. "Shit, shit, shit," she whispered in a panic and gathered up her wallet, the small packet of Kleenex, her keys, and the little hairspray can that she carried always when in Los Angeles. She had hoped she wouldn't need it here, but better safe than sorry. It was then she noticed a Ziploc bag. Sarah picked it up. Her breath quickened. Something sharp and cold tore into her stomach. She was not an authority on the subject, but she knew this was cocaine. Charles? No way. He just didn't seem the type to be involved with drugs. But what did she know. In the past, she had been deceived by people she trusted. She replaced the bag where she found it, grabbed her purse and prayed that Charles wouldn't come back and catch her. Sarah peeked into the hallway. All clear. She made her way to the elevator, almost knocking over a woman carrying an ice bucket. For a moment, she thought she recognized her, but the baseball hat and dark glasses covered most of her face. She calmed down, pressed the elevator button, then glanced back. She saw the woman enter a room. *Was that Charles' room or the one next door?* She hesitated and watched until the woman left the room. She was carrying what looked like a plastic bag. Sarah thought about what she had seen in Charles's room. *No, it has to be a coincidence. I'm just being paranoid.* As the elevator arrived and the doors slid open, she stepped inside. Glancing back one last time, she noticed the woman had already disappeared.

In the lobby, Harry was reading a newspaper but looked up to greet Sarah.

"Sorry I snapped at you this morning," she said.

"No problem—I just thought that you guys were, you know, getting along well and..."

Sarah blushed.

"I'd better shut up. Sorry, it was insensitive of me," Harry added.

That comment was out of character, she thought, then said, "Any sign of Charles?"

Harry put down the newspaper. "He left a note for me. Said he had to attend to some business and got off to an early start. He's such a mysterious chap sometimes."

They chatted for a while, mainly about the weather and local food.

Sarah looked at her watch. "I must get going. I have to vacate my room."

"You're not leaving Mexico, are you?" queried Harry.

"No, today I'm moving into a ranch just close to the Hilton Hotel."

"Ranchero Castillo?"

"Yes," said Sarah. "How do you know about it?"

"Just passed by it the other day on the way to the Rent-a-Car place."

"It's a beautiful ranch," said Sarah.

"There's a lot of wonderful ranches and villas in this area, although most need major renovations," said Harry.

Sarah rose from the chair. "Well, I'll see you later. I'll leave word for Charles of my whereabouts."

She went to her old room and packed up her belongings. The maid would have to do the clean up, so she left a ten-dollar bill on the bedside table. The Mexicans loved receiving American dollars. She wondered how Harry knew about the ranch—not many tourists go that way. All the tourist sights and clubs were in the other direction, as was the Rent-a-car place. She asked herself, Am I over reacting? Maybe Harry is just more adventurous, traveling farther out than most tourists. Two hours later, she was relaxing on the patio of her new living quarters, drinking a Tequila sunrise.

'Suddenly, she felt strong hands on her shoulders, thumbs pressing into her tight and tired muscles, which sent tingles through her body. Sensual thoughts rushed to her mind. She could recognize his touch anytime, anywhere.

"That feels wonderful," she purred. His hands moved down her back gradually as he removed the flimsy top and unfastened her bra. The straps fell over her arms. His strong hands moved down to her breasts. He turned her gently around and lowered his lips to hers.

The kiss was passionate. He picked her up and took her to his room. As she lay on the bed, he slowly undressed'.

Sarah let the book drop into her lap and laid her head back, allowing romantic daydreams to carry her away. A few minutes later, she opened her eyes, looked up, and saw *Senora* Magdelena. "You sleeping?" she asked.

Blushing, Sarah stammered, "No, just daydreaming."

Senora Magdelena informed her that Ricardo was on a business trip, and she should make herself at home, and she could borrow the old truck to drive into town.

She was curious that both Charles and Ricardo had to leave on business at the same time. *Just another coincidence?* She finished her drink, another chapter of her book, and took a drive into town. Sarah never considered herself the typical tourist but enjoyed walks down the less traveled streets. She observed a doorway that looked like a hundred others, but a small sign in Spanish indicated a restaurant. The door was cut into a brown adobe wall from which the whitewash had flaked off long ago. It led into a courtyard with a redbrick floor. All kinds of fruit trees whitewashed five feet up the trunk stood like soldiers against the back wall. She sat and ordered from a waiter wearing black trousers, black shirt, a starched white apron, and a wonderful smile.

Sarah sipped a martini, quite strong and a little too sweet. Other tables were filled with locals; she was the only *gringa.* Noises from the street were only a faint, eerie echo in the background. A cool breeze carried the scent of the orange blossoms from nearby trees. She sighed and scrolled through pictures on her phone. She stopped at the shots of her and Charles at the ruins and smiled to herself. They really had fun that day even though it ended with danger. One of the photos would have been ideal, except for the presence of a rather dubious-looking character lingering in the background. She ordered another drink, leisurely scanning her surroundings. People-watching was her favorite pastime, so she was in no hurry to leave. A peculiar noise caught her attention, prompting her to turn around and witness the entrance of two wiry chickens. They surveyed the other tables before scurrying in her direction. Without hesitation, she shared some bread with the unexpected guests and quickly reached for her phone to capture the amusing moment. The waiters carried on as if such occurrences were entirely routine in this unique setting.

Sarah walked back to the truck and drove to the ranch. She couldn't stop thinking about Charles and what she had seen in his room. She enjoyed reading mystery novels but didn't appreciate being in the middle of one. Nothing so far made sense. A swirl of conflicting emotions enveloped her, and now she wished that she could erase the night they had spent together. That was not like her—casual sex.

She couldn't wait until Ricardo called so she could tell him everything that had happened in the past twenty-four hours. Maybe he could give her some answers. *Maybe I should go home... but no! No one is going to ruin my vacation. All these maybes!* She was munching on some leftover tacos when Ricardo called. As her story unfolded, his voice trembled with anger, and he told her he would return to the ranch as soon as possible. Meanwhile, she should stay close to home. She replaced the phone on the cradle, pleased that he sounded genuinely concerned.

Sarah realized she liked Ricardo but not romantically, more as a friend or big brother. He was like the older brother she never had. He was so caring, but at the same time, he was rather distant. He didn't allow himself to get too close. If only he would talk more about his family, but she understood the grief he was carrying.

She thought about the drugs she had seen in Charles' room. Questions loomed in her mind. Ricardo had told her to stay at the ranch, but she needed to clear her head. She remembered that *Senora* Magdelena had mentioned earlier about the horses, so she changed into some comfortable clothes and walked to the stables. She approached Santos, the stable hand, and asked him to saddle up his most reliable horse for her. He led out a chestnut with white fetlocks and gentle eyes. "*Senorita, esta* Maria. She *muy bueno*. Good horse. Good horse."

"Thank you," replied Sarah, mounting. "I won't be long."

She kicked her heels for a gentle trot, getting used to the American saddle, and once she felt at ease, flicked the reins and clicked her tongue, sending the steed into a full gallop through the countryside, avoiding the bare branches. Her hair blew in the wind as her mind finally cleared of all bad thoughts. She felt the exhilaration rush through her body. She slowed down and continued up a hilly road until it came to a dead end. She dismounted, tied Maria to a tree, grabbed her bag, and sat to admire the spectacular view of the town below. She had packed a tuna sandwich and can of orange juice. The cloudless blue sky, green hills, and a glimpse of the ocean set her mind at ease. But when a crackle of a dry twig disturbed her thoughts. Sarah turned quickly. "Who's there?" No answer. She looked around. Nothing. Then another breaking twig. Sarah again shouted, "Who's there?"

Just then, a rabbit appeared, looked at her, and took off. Sarah laughed with relief. A measure of calm returned. Her breathing slowed, and she lay down, feeling the warm sun on her face. A few minutes later, a shadow blocked out the sunlight. She opened her eyes, shading them with her hand. She sat up quickly. "Hello."

The man didn't answer and just stared at Sarah. He stood over her.

Sarah stood up quickly, grabbing her bag. "Who are you? What are you doing here?"

He was a short, scruffy Mexican with a bad complexion, a '50s greased-back hairdo, and an angry expression. She realized she stood at least six inches taller than him, which made her feel a little more confident.

"Do you speak English?" she asked as she rummaged around her bag for the mini hairspray.

"Where eez de package?" he demanded.

"What package?" she yelled back. "What the hell is going on? Who are you? What do you want?"

"Hey! I ask de questions. Tell me where's de package?"

"I have no idea what you're talking about."

He moved closer and grabbed her arm. Reacting swiftly, Sarah grasped the can of hair spray firmly and, without hesitation, unleashed a stream directly into his eyes. The man howled in pain, cursing and rubbing his eyes with his pudgy fingers. Seizing the opportunity, Sarah broke free and dashed towards the waiting horse. She untied the reins, vaulted into the saddle, and spurred the horse into a gallop, leaving the commotion behind in a cloud of dust.

Sarah had stayed out longer than expected, and when she dropped the horse back in the deserted barn, Santos and *Senora* Magdelena came running out yelling, *"Esta bien*, Ju okay, *senorita?* If anything happen to you, Signor Castillo, he fire me."

She took a deep breath and calmly said, "I'm fine, *senora*. I went further than I intended to, and now I'm late. I have to go into town to see a friend. Can I borrow the truck? I'll be back soon."

"Please be careful, *senorita*."

11

As Sarah drove into town, her hands trembled as they gripped the steering wheel. The man she encountered left her unsettled. He seemed oddly familiar. She thought hard, and the memory clicked—she had seen him at the ranch, engaged in conversation with Ricardo. Questions flooded her mind. Who was Ricardo, and what was his involvement in all this? Then she remembered the *senora* had called him *Senor* Castillo when his name was Sanchez. *Was he lying to me about his identity? Why? What did he have to hide from me?*

She glanced in the rear-view mirror. Only a gray Toyota was close behind her. She accelerated, and so did the Toyota. Was she being followed? The Toyota sped towards her. Just as the car was about to hit her, it swerved past, and a youth gave her the finger.

I'm going crazy. I'm starting to imagine things, thought Sarah.

She parked the truck haphazardly in front of Charles' hotel. Luckily, she didn't have to go far, as he was at the bar chatting with Sylvia and Harry. She quickly walked over to them as Charles said, "Sarah, darling, where have you been?"

"I need to talk to you—alone," she replied.

They left Harry as he flirted with Sylvia. "I was worried about you. I didn't see you at all yesterday," said Charles.

"I needed some time alone."

"Sarah, I want you to know I enjoy your company very much, and I was afraid you might still think there was a romance going on with Sylvia, but there isn't. I... I like you."

Sarah forced a smile at Charles.

"I mean... "

"Not now, Charles. I need to tell you something. I went out for a horseback ride today." Her breathing increased, and she could hear her own heartbeat as the realization that she had been in a very dangerous situation hit her hard.

Charles held her hands. "What on earth happened to you?"

"I was approached by a man who looked vaguely familiar. I think I had seen him talking to Ricardo. He kept asking me where the package was. I had absolutely no idea what he was referring to. I think I need to file a police report. Would you come with me?"

"Of course, but I also think it's time you left the ranch. You need to come back to the hotel. Did the man try to hurt you?"

Sarah gave a nervous laugh. "He grabbed my arm, but before he could do anything, I sprayed him with my hair spray."

Charles laughed. "Blimey! You never fail to surprise me! I wonder if his eyelashes are still stuck together."

Sarah relaxed and smiled at the cockney term, which was a little out of character for Charles.

"Well, let's go," he said.

He yelled to Harry and Sylvia that he was going on an errand with Sarah and left before either of them could respond. They walked about a block, turned down a quiet street, and stopped in front of a dilapidated building.

"They don't have much of a budget for the police or fire

department in this town," said Charles.

"I guess not," said Sarah as she looked at the broken stone wall and the peeling paint on the entry door. They pushed it open and Sarah walked up to the desk. The uniformed policeman smiled and asked in Spanish how he could help. Charles hovered in the background. "I'm sorry, do you speak English?" asked Sarah.

"Of course. How can I help you?"

Sarah explained what happened, and he looked at her curiously. "Did we not meet at the hotel when your room was broken into?"

"Yes," said Sarah.

"*Senorita*, you seem to be attracting a lot of problems."

"It would seem that way."

He made Sarah feel uncomfortable, especially when he said something in Spanish to another policeman, and they laughed. He wrote down the details and said he would pass it on to his detective. Sarah walked towards Charles. "They'll probably throw it in the trash as soon as I leave."

"Stay here," said Charles as he walked to the desk.

Sarah couldn't hear the hushed chatter, but she saw Charles pull out his wallet. Oh, my God, thought Sarah. she had heard about *la mordida*, the term used for bribery in this country, but never thought she would see it in action. The desk cop sat up and nodded to Charles.

Charles took Sarah by the arm, and they walked back to the hotel.

"I don't think those guys believed me," said Sarah. "They acted so bloody macho. It pissed me off. I need a drink, like a double Scotch."

"Don't worry, I had a little chat with them."

"How much did that cost you?" asked Sarah.

Charles just laughed. Back at the hotel, they sat in a corner away from the crowd gathering for evening cocktails. Sarah watched him go to the bar and order the drinks. *Surely he's not involved with drugs. There must be some explanation.*

Charles returned with a double Scotch in each hand. Sarah looked around. Harry and Sylvia were nowhere to be seen. It had been a rough day, but Sarah's adrenaline kept her going. Even after another double Scotch, she still felt wide awake.

They sat in a comfortable silence until Sarah plucked up the courage to ask Charles about the drugs. "Charles, I do have to ask you something."

"Yes?"

"Where were you Sunday morning?"

"I needed to attend to some business."

"All night?"

"What are you talking about?"

"I woke up at 4am and you were gone. I went to your room as I thought you were sleeping, so I came to wake you, and your bed hadn't been slept in."

"I'm sorry I missed that. I enjoyed our intimate evening together, and..."

"Don't change the subject," she snapped.

"I told you; I had to attend to some business."

He sounded so genuine she wanted to believe him. "I am totally confused and don't know who I can trust."

"Please trust me. I can't explain anything at the moment."

"But, Charles, I know about the drugs," she blurted.

"What drugs?"

"As I was saying, I came to your room, saw the drugs, and that's when I dropped my purse."

"Your purse?"

"My bag, whatever you want to call it. I left in a hurry, so I must have lost my gold lighter. I don't suppose you happened to see it anywhere?"

"I'll tell you right now, there were no drugs in my room, and there never will be. I'll look again, but I don't recall seeing any lighter either."

"How can I believe you?"

"Why would I lie to you? I'm trying to impress you, not chase you away."

"Okay. Let's talk about it later. I really need to get my things from the ranch and move back to the hotel. I'm not sure if I trust Ricardo anymore."

"I should come with you," said Charles.

"No, I don't want Ricardo to get suspicious."

Sarah drove back to the ranch and had a short, restless sleep. Next morning, she grabbed her belongings and silently slipped into the hallway, closing the door behind her. She heard Ricardo's voice so scuttled down the back stairs to avoid him. She didn't want to wait for a cab, so borrowed Ricardo's truck with intentions to return it later. Shaking, she turned the key in the ignition, then again and again. Nothing. *Come on, you piece of shit. Start.*

A hand appeared on the rolled-down window. Sarah gasped. It was Ricardo.

"Where are you going? I need to talk to you."

"I can't. I have an... er... appointment, and I'm already late," she said, turning the key once more.

"Well, this old truck is not going to get you very far. You've flooded the engine. Also, there is a little matter I have to discuss with you."

His frame filled the whole opening as he leaned in the window. Sarah withdrew and shrank back. His tone of voice was serious. *Did he know about her visit to the cops and how she had mentioned him?* "Well, in that case, I guess I have no choice,"

She was glad he had not noticed her suitcase on the floor of the truck. Once inside the villa, she sat silently while the *senora* entered with a tray of coffee and croissants.

"Thank you, *senora*," said Ricardo, then turned to Sarah.

"So, I had a little chat with the local police. Seems you or your English friend said that I had something to do with the man who threatened you. Tell me more."

Sarah told him about the incident when she was out riding. "But, Ricardo," she hesitated, "I had seen the same guy talking to you at the ranch. And another thing, the *senora* called you Castillo."

"Ah! That is why I was questioned. I really don't appreciate you spreading rumors about me. It's ridiculous. I know a lot of people in this town. I don't even know who you are referring to," he scowled.

"What's going on, Ricardo? What are you doing here? You told me you were on family business. You told me your friend and your brother were both dead. Where's the rest of your family? Something's not adding up, and I feel like I'm being played."

"All I can tell you is it's true; my real name is Ricardo Castillo, and this ranch belongs to me, and I work for the DEA. The reason I came here is that my brother was killed a few months ago in Los Angeles. He was lead investigator with the Agency, so I can't tell you much more, as I don't want to put you in danger."

"Your brother? What was his name?"

"Juan Carlos, but he called himself John. He was working undercover and following a lead on a drug cartel."

Sarah gasped. She thought it was just a coincidence that he was called John. "And he was working in Los Angeles?"

"Yes, why?"

Sarah described her John: "He called himself John Castle!"

"God! That sounds like him. How did you know him?"

"If it was my John, I met him over six months ago, and we had a beautiful relationship. Then he just disappeared on me."

Ricardo pulled out a photo. "Is this him?"

"Oh, my God! Yes."

Sarah gazed at him, her eyes welling up with tears. "I thought it was a genuine relationship, but when he disappeared, I convinced myself it must have just been a fling."

"Sarah, I'm so sorry," Ricardo empathized. "At least now you know why he never returned your calls. He did mention to me that he had met someone wonderful but never disclosed a name."

"He really said that?" a mix of emotions flooded her body.

"Yes, he was sincere," Ricardo confirmed.

Sarah managed a weak smile, forcing back the tears. How did she ever doubt his feelings for her? Her gaze dropped to the floor, avoiding eye contact with Ricardo, and a heavy silence settled between them. She felt a slight quiver on her lips as she tried to say something. Ricardo gave her a gentle hug until her tears subsided, then continued, his tone somber. "I got a call from the Agency. He had been shot. Did he ever mention anything about his meetings?"

"No. He was always evasive when I asked him what kind of work he did. He used to joke and tell me he was a spy. I guess not so much a joke now. He never talked about his family or friends either, so there was no one I could call when I hadn't heard from him."

"The less you knew, the better. But usually, he never dated while he was undercover. You must have been very special."

They sat in silence. Sarah's mind wandered back to the time they had spent on the yacht. She thought she would never ever meet anyone like him again. When she felt she had regained her composure, she said, "I did like him very much. In fact, I loved him."

"I'm sorry, but I have to ask: what else happened with that guy who threatened you?" said Ricardo.

"He kept talking about some package. I had no idea what he was talking about." Her voice rose almost to a wail.

Again, Ricardo reached out to calm her. "Look, you need to trust me. Unfortunately, I think our friend Carmen, who is a little jealous of you, probably told the wrong people that you were the one who stole some drugs from them, and they believed her. I will have to pay a visit to her uncle to clear this up."

"Is she and her family involved in drug dealing?"

"I can't say right now. Rumor is that the international ringleader is believed to be English."

"English? That's weird. Wait a minute. You don't think Charles has something to do with all this?"

Ricardo just shrugged his shoulders. "Sorry, Sarah, I can't tell you anything else. The less you know, the safer you are. I have a meeting to go to now. I'll talk with you a little later."

Sarah sighed. "I just wish this was all over so I could relax and play tourist."

Ricardo hugged her gently. Sarah realized he was one of the good guys.

"When this is all over, you should come back as my guest for a real relaxing holiday."

"That's very kind of you."

"So, you have definitely decided to go back to the hotel?" asked Ricardo.

"Yes, I will feel a little safer in town. I called the hotel, and they do have a room for me."

Sarah finished her coffee and wiped away her tears, thankful that nothing romantic had happened between her and Ricardo. *Charles, a drug dealer. No way.* She really couldn't accept the fact that Charles was on the wrong side of the law, especially dealing drugs.

Once again, she thought about John and what a strange coincidence all this was. She grabbed her luggage from the truck and called a taxi to return to the hotel. She had to give Charles the benefit of the doubt. The taxi arrived within ten minutes. The driver took her case and placed it in the trunk as she settled in the back seat, her mind in a confused state.

Following the conversation with Sarah, Charles returned to his hotel room. He meticulously searched every corner, yet there were no traces of any drugs or a lighter. Why would Sarah fabricate such a story? What motivated Ricardo to plant such ideas in her mind? Determined to unravel the mystery, he believed it was time to meet up with Ricardo and set things straight.

12

As Sarah lay on the sun-drenched beach, the rhythmic sound of the waves washing ashore provided a soothing backdrop to her contemplation. She closed her eyes, allowing the warmth of the sun to ease the tension in her body.

Thoughts swirled in her mind like seagulls in the sky above. Ricardo's involvement with Carmen was now clear, but had she stolen the drugs and then told her uncle that Sarah was the one who took them? How childish. How did *Don* Manuel or his men know what Sarah looked like and where to find her? She now knew Ricardo was trying to protect her. Charles, on the other hand, was becoming more enigmatic by the day with his frequent meetings, but he had sounded confused when Sarah mentioned the drugs in his room. Sarah wondered if there was more to him than met the eye. And Harry's presence added another layer of complexity to the situation. There was something about Harry she didn't trust. Lost in thought, Sarah realized that she needed to trust her instincts, just as she had learned to do during her travels and adventures.

As the sun continued to warm her skin, she decided to relax and clear her mind. She turned onto her back, closed her eyes, and was almost asleep when a shadow clouded her face. She squinted and opened one eye. Harry stood over her. She looked up at him, regaining her composure, and said, "Hello, haven't seen you in a while. I was just thinking about you."

"I hope they were good thoughts," he replied. "Mind if I join you?"

"It's a public beach," she replied a little sarcastically.

"You don't like me very much, do you?"

Sarah blushed and stammered. "I... er... don't know you that well."

"That's because you give all your attention to Charles. By the way, have you seen him lately?"

"Not since last night in the bar."

"You really like him, don't you?" asked Harry.

"I think he's a very interesting and caring person—but you should know, you have known him a long time."

"Oh, yes, we go back many years. He was the one who always excelled in everything, especially with the women."

"Do I detect a little jealousy?"

"Probably. I've always been jealous of him and always will be. I remember once in England, we were in this club, and I fancied this girl. I went and bought her a drink, and she joined us. Charles immediately started to flirt with her, so I got drunk and left. That was Sylvia! I heard they spent a whole week in a Paris hotel. I didn't see either of them after that until I arrived here. When I saw Charles, I just thought it was a strange coincidence. But it's an old hangout from our student days. We used to come here to learn Spanish, but I never picked it up like Charles did. Then, out of the blue, Sylvia shows up."

"Charles told me there was nothing between them. Why should he lie?" asked Sarah.

"Charles lies a lot," said Harry, laughing.

"Why are you talking such rubbish?"

"Well, I am not lying when I tell you your boyfriend is married."

Sarah knew her face could not hide the hurt she felt. She bit her lip, controlling her anger.

"He's not my boyfriend. Can't a girl have male friends without being accused of sleeping with them?"

"Don't give me that crap. I've seen the way you and Charles look at each other. He's damn lucky to have such a beautiful wife, and then, what does he do? Comes over here and flirts with any attractive girl he meets."

"Harry, you're just jealous. I've had enough of this conversation, and I'm burning up. Goodbye!" Sarah grabbed her towel and stormed off.

Harry called out, "Yeah. I think my sensitive skin is crying out for aloe vera." He caught up with her and asked, "Are you still staying at the villa?"

"No, it was too far away from everything. I'm back at the hotel now," she replied cautiously. Maybe I'll see you later. *Ciao.*"

She decided to spend the evening alone and write some postcards.

'At that moment, she heard the glass crack, and a strange pain went through her side. She didn't realize she had been shot until she felt the warm blood trickle down her leg. Everything became fuzzy, and that's all she remembered until she opened her eyes in a strange hospital. The pain was excruciating. She pressed a buzzer, and a nurse came in.

"Finally, you're awake."

"How long have I been out," she asked.

"Twelve hours," answered the nurse, looking at her watch. "Can you tell me what happened?"

12

A crash of thunder brought Sarah back to reality. She laughed. Between her book and everything she had experienced, she could write her own novel when she arrived home.

It was about ten p.m. and it began to rain. Slowly at first, and then it broke into one of those unexpected torrential storms. The lightning flashed, casting an eerie light across her room. The temperature cooled down, and the wind struck up, blowing the shutters against the wall. Another clap of thunder, louder than any explosion, shot angrily against the sky. Then something crashed. The curtains had knocked a vase onto the ground, and it shattered into pieces. Sarah got up, switched on the lamp by her bed and closed the window, avoiding the shattered pieces. The lights went out.

"Damn," she muttered and picked up her mobile phone. Once again, she swore. She had forgotten to plug in the charger. In the darkness, she inched her way across the room. It reminded her of the experience of the earthquake back in L.A. She had been woken up at four a.m. with no candles or flashlight to see her way out. All the china in the kitchen had flown out of the cupboards and was in pieces on the floor. The other tenants of the building were outside, but it happened to be a cold night, so Sarah just climbed back into bed, thinking, *If I am going to die, I may as well die in bed.*

She went back to bed, but her busy mind refused to let her sleep. After ten more minutes of restless tossing and turning, she gave up and decided to search for some candles. She crept down the stairs on her butt. On the floor below, she stopped and sat still on a small landing. Voices were coming up the stairwell. They were speaking in Spanish, and one of the voices sounded familiar but not native to the language. Trying to get closer, she bumped into a table.

"*Quien es?* Who's there?"

"Just me, Sarah," she said as a flashlight swung up and shone in her face. She stood up and hung over the banister. A dim light from the window helped her recognize Pedro, the night manager.

"Do you need something?" he asked angrily.

"Candles. And for God's sake, get that light out of my eyes. I am a paying guest."

"We don't have any, so please go back to your room. I have enough problems calming the other guests."

"Are you alone?" she asked.

"Of course."

"I could have sworn I heard someone else down there. I know you must have candles, or at least give me a flashlight so I can return to my room safely."

"Wait there." He returned quickly with another flashlight and threw it to Sarah, who almost dropped it. "Now, go back to your room."

Sarah grabbed the flashlight and shone it back down on Pedro. He was alone. She slowly climbed back up to her room. She wondered why Pedro lied to her. She knew she had heard more than one person speaking. As the lights came back on, she looked out of her window and saw a white SUV driving towards town. She couldn't see the driver but wondered who it could be. She crawled back under the covers and fell into a restless sleep.

At seven a.m., she met Charles for breakfast.

"What are you going to do today?" said Charles. He looked like he hadn't slept much.

"Maybe I'll go visit some ruins, get kidnapped, or go into town and get mugged."

"Very funny," he said dryly.

12

"Did you know, last night during the storm, I went downstairs for candles, and in the darkness, I heard voices. But Pedro insisted he was alone. I know I heard another person. It was a familiar voice too. Definitely didn't sound like a local."

"Did you understand anything?" asked Charles, looking concerned.

"No, I was too busy concentrating on not falling down the damn stairs."

"Too bad; there's something about Pedro I don't trust. You be careful around him."

"Okay. Does Harry Whelan speak Spanish?" asked Sarah.

"He told me he could never get the hang of the language when we used to come here during our college days. It probably wasn't him. What does it matter?

"Just curious." Why is Charles acting so vague? she thought but didn't pursue the conversation any further.

"You enjoy your day. Gotta run. I have a meeting. When I get back I will be able to explain everything to you." He kissed her on the cheek and hurried off.

Why can't I meet a normal guy? But then it would be boring, she thought, smiling.

13

A few miles down the road, Ricardo entered the San Antonio Ranch. Don Manuel was unaware of Ricardo's connection to the federal agency and had eagerly accepted him to be part of the drug cartel. He knew Ricardo's family from many years ago, so had no reason not to trust him. Ricardo had asked Manuel not to mention his connection to his family.

It was only after his brother's death that Ricardo was made aware of Manuel's drug business. He wasn't surprised, as he often wondered where Manuel got all his money. The DEA had sent him to investigate. So, this meeting was the big one. Capos and street enforcers from all the syndicates would be there. Armed guards carrying AK-47s stood like sentries at all the exits. It would be a great day for everyone if all these guys were put behind bars. He thought about his brother. Revenge is sweet. He had to stay calm.

He walked through the old iron doors into a house lavishly furnished. This was the place where Manuel conducted most of his business. The constant tick of a grandfather clock dominated the room. The heavy, ornate décor clashed with the gritty world of drug dealing. The room was abuzz with chatter in a distinct Spanish dialect, which hinted at connections to South American cartels, possibly Colombian. However, the one person he was looking for, the elusive Englishman, was conspicuously absent.

Ricardo's phone alerted him with a beep, and he discreetly stepped out of the room. With a sense of urgency, he sent a text message to his contact in the Bureau, providing an update on the situation and detailing the individuals he had encountered but warned them that the Englishman was not in the room. He walked back inside and helped himself to a coffee when a maid asked, "Would you like a cocktail, *senor*?"

"*Non, gracias.*" He had to keep a clear head and stay alert, knowing it would all be over soon. He scoured the room and couldn't help but feel a sense of unease. He had been undercover a few years back but never imagined that he would have to repeat that kind of work. He had retired early from the agency and enjoyed his time playing golf, going to the gym and just hanging out with his buddies. He thought he may even meet someone he could settle down with. Right now, he had to tread carefully to ensure his own safety.

As everyone settled at the table, Manuel apologized about a certain person not being present, and Ricardo realized he was referring to the Englishman in question. Ricardo kept a close eye on Manuel's associates, looking for any signs of suspicious behavior or clues that could lead him closer to the truth about his brother's murderer. In his eyes, all these people looked like they could shoot anyone without a second's hesitation. He detested them all but was determined to uncover the truth. He was disappointed that the Englishman had not showed up, but hoped the DEA would track the guy down with help from MI6—the foreign Intelligence service in the UK.

Amidst the opulent surroundings of the meeting room, the atmosphere was heavy with tension as the power players of the criminal underworld delved into the intricacies of their drug operations. Names, places, and vast sums of money were mentioned as they charted out their distribution networks and smuggling routes. Each leader was acutely aware of the stakes involved, with millions of dollars hanging in the balance, and the possible threat of law enforcement. The room reverberated with whispered promises and the unspoken understanding that their ruthless world operated on the edge between wealth and ruin.

Two hours passed, and the meeting was over. As the attendees continued to socialize, knocking back shots of expensive Tequila, oblivious to the danger that lay ahead, Ricardo waited for the response from his contact. He knew that time was of the essence, and every second counted in this high-stakes game.

In the early evening, a convoy of unmarked DEA vehicles, their headlights off, approached the target location of Don Manuel's villa on the outskirts of the city. Special agents, armed to the teeth, moved swiftly and silently. The agents had meticulously planned this raid for days, gathering intelligence, tracking suspects, and securing search warrants.

As they reached the villa's fortified entrance, chaos erupted. Smoke grenades filled the air with blinding light and deafening noise, disorienting the criminals within. A few shots were fired. Swiftly and methodically, agents moved through the building, clearing rooms, and apprehending suspects. Outside, local law enforcement provided crucial perimeter security, ensuring that no one escaped. Within a short time, the mission was accomplished, and the criminals were in custody.

Charles made a beeline for Manuel. He knocked him to the floor and wrapped the handcuffs tightly round his wrists.

13

Manuel screamed, "You will regret this."

"Don't be so sure of yourself. You've ordered the deaths of so many people. This is not personal, but I'll do whatever it takes to make sure you are behind bars for life, or believe me, I'll put you in your fucking grave."

To avoid suspicion, Ricardo was handcuffed by an agent. Charles walked over to him and whispered, "So, no Harry?"

"No," replied Ricardo, "If he was here and recognized me, he would have left, but I'm pretty sure he didn't know I was working with you guys. Either way, he obviously didn't want me to see him here."

"Well, he can't be too far away," said Charles.

"I don't know. He's always one step ahead of us," said Ricardo.

Charles turned to an agent, "You get these guys locked up, and I'll finish up here. Then, I'm going to find that son of a bitch, Harry Whelan. Thanks. Your cooperation made a huge difference today."

Ricardo said, with a mixture of relief and sadness in his eyes, "I hope this brings some closure for my brother's death."

Charles nodded sympathetically. "We'll do everything we can to ensure that those responsible for his murder face justice."

As the sun began to set over the Mexican landscape, Ricardo and Charles stood together, knowing that their combined efforts had dealt a significant blow to the criminal underworld, but for Ricardo, the pain of losing his brother would always linger.

14

Sarah was in good spirits as she strolled through the hotel lobby. Charles had been excited when he left her, mentioning something about explaining everything that had happened. He had said he would catch up with her later, and they would celebrate. So, she went shopping and walked along the boardwalk, the sea breeze playing with her hair and the sound of waves calming her thoughts.

As she browsed through the boutiques, picking up a few souvenirs and treating herself to a new dress, her mind wandered back to Charles' words. Despite the pleasant distraction, she couldn't shake off the curiosity and slight apprehension. What could have possibly made him so excited to share? *What was he referring to? The drugs, the incident with the falling rocks, Ricardo?* Whatever it was, she couldn't wait to see him again. However there was that little matter of him being married. *Was Harry lying?*

There were very few people around; most of them were down by the sea or sitting by their hotel pool, as it was a very hot day. To escape the heat and bright sunshine, she bought an ice cream and sat on a bench shaded by a tall palm tree. She quickly devoured the vanilla ice cream as it trickled down her hand. A shadow covered her face. She looked up. It was a young woman, and she spoke to Sarah in Spanish.

"Sorry, my Spanish is not that good."

"Oh, no problem. I speak a little English. May I sit down?"

"Of course," said Sarah, feeling a little uncomfortable. She eyed her shabby clothes and noticed a faint smell of alcohol.

"Ice cream is good, *si*?"

"*Si*. Would you like me to buy you one?"

"Oh, no, thank you. I just need to sit for a while."

Sarah tried to think of a good exit. "Well, excuse me, I need to go to the restroom to wash my hands." Sarah stood up, threw the small piece of cone in the trash, and said goodbye to this strange woman.

"Enjoy your day, *senora*."

"You too, *senorita*."

Sarah walked into the public bathroom, holding her nose from the stench. She would never use the toilets, even washing her hands was a challenge with the small trickle of water from the tap and the empty soap dispenser. There was also a faint odor that reminded her of a hospital. Before she knew it, the woman had followed her unnoticed and gagged Sarah with a strange smelling cloth. Sarah felt dizzy, and that was the last she remembered until she awoke.

When she came to, she was in an unfamiliar room. The walls were bare, and the only light came from a dim bulb hanging from the ceiling. Her head throbbed, and her mouth was as dry as the Sahara Desert. She tried to move but her hands were tied behind her back. Panic started to set in, but she forced herself to stay calm. The room was small and sparsely furnished, with only a chair and a table in the corner. She strained her ears for any sound but heard nothing apart from her own breathing and the faint hum of the light bulb. The air was cool, carrying a musty scent, suggesting she might be in a basement or a similar secluded area.

She took a deep breath, trying to steady her pounding heartbeat. Her thoughts raced back to Charles and what he had said earlier. Was this related to the secrets he was so eager to reveal? And where was he now? She had so many questions, but for now, her priority was to find a way out of this predicament.

"Welcome to my humble abode," said a familiar voice.

Sarah strained her eyes in the dark room and saw an outline of a figure approaching her. "Who are you?" she thought, the voice sounded familiar.

"It's me, my dear."

The figure came into her sight, pointing a gun to her face. It *was* Harry Whelan.

"I thought we should spend some time together," he said sarcastically.

"Well, a gun can prove very persuasive, especially when you're looking at it from this end," retorted Sarah, her voice shaking.

"Always the comedienne," replied Harry.

"Have you gone mad, or is this a practical joke?" she said, feeling more anger than fear.

"No joke, darling. Your boyfriend is interfering with my business. I just need some leverage to get him to back off. So, when he comes to rescue you, it will give me the time I need to attend to some unfinished business and get away from this Godforsaken place."

At that moment, there was a knock on the door. "Come in!" shouted Harry.

It was Pedro, the manager from the hotel.

Damn, Ricardo warned me about that son of a bitch. What if

Charles and Ricardo don't find me? What's going to happen to me? I don't think I can talk my way out of this one.

Pedro exchanged a few words in Spanish with Harry and left.

"You told me you couldn't speak Spanish," exclaimed Sarah.

"I lied," he said.

"What else did you lie about?" said Sarah, gritting her teeth.

Harry smiled. "You may find out one day. For now, don't give me any trouble, and no harm will come to you. Charles is my enemy. You are a mere pawn in this game. However, just to prove I'm not all bad, I'll send you some food later. I have a little errand to run." With that, he left.

Sarah's head throbbed and she felt sick. She felt angry. Charles should have told her she might be in danger. Why had he left her in the dark about the risks? If she had known, she would have been more cautious. Her thoughts kept circling back to the cryptic excitement in Charles' eyes when he mentioned explaining everything. Did he know this could happen? Had he underestimated the danger?

Thirty minutes later, Pedro appeared with a tray of food. Sarah looked at it. "What's that crap?"

"It's good Mexican food. You be grateful!" Pedro placed the tray on an empty crate in front of her and untied her hands. Sarah was tempted to hit him, but it wouldn't accomplish much.

"You eat! Don't try to escape, or I will tie you like a pig! I come back later."

Sarah stared after him as he bolted the door. Her fear turned to outrage, and hatred welled up inside of her, towards Harry and anyone else connected with him. "Bastard!" she screamed to the empty room.

What if the food is poisoned? Or has drugs in it. Or am I being over dramatic?

As those unsettling thoughts crossed her mind, a wave of fear extinguished her hunger. With her hands free, she seized the chance to look around the room. It was better than sitting like a scared rabbit. The windows were nailed shut. She peered through the obscured glass, straining to recognize her surroundings, but to no avail. The door was bolted, yet hope flickered as approached another door. The rotten wooden slats caught her attention. She bent over and, summoning all her strength, she gripped one of the wooden slats. To her surprise, it broke away. Grateful for the assistance of termites or any unseen creatures that had feasted on the aged wood, she silently thanked them. She continued extracting more slats. Each piece she removed opened the gap wide enough for her to scramble through, which allowed her to crawl into a hallway beyond.

As she crept along, she stole a glance through a window to survey her surroundings. The eerie silence persisted, and there were no signs of anyone around. Had she found a way out?

Back at the San Antonio ranch, Charles and the other agents finished searching the entire house. The Mexican police drove off with Manuel and his men.

"Just leave Senor Ricardo with my men. We're not finished with him yet!" Charles instructed.

When everyone had gone, Charles unlocked Ricardo's handcuffs and turned to him. "Even after our meeting together, I thought there was a chance you may still be involved with these guys."

Ricardo laughed heartily. "Yup. Even though you told me about Harry, I still had suspicions of you being the head honcho. I even told Sarah that! Maybe you need to find her and straighten things out."

Charles wore a genuine smile. "I'll go now. I really like her. I'm seriously considering transferring to the US and joining the FBI. Maybe I could opt for a regular job, but honestly, I'd miss all this excitement," he mused. Pausing for a moment, his expression turned more serious. "However, finding Harry is our priority. You're welcome to come back with us."

"Thanks, but I have someone I need to see. It's going to be tough telling Carmen about her uncle."

"Was she aware of his illegal business?" Charles inquired.

Ricardo sighed. "She's a smart girl, so I'm certain she had her suspicions. In fact, I think it was her who stole the drugs and then planted some in your room," he admitted.

Perplexed, Charles questioned, "But why would she do that?"

Ricardo explained, "She knew that if she made Sarah suspicious of you, she would probably leave Mexico. She felt threatened, thinking that I might also be interested in Sarah.

"Did you have feelings for Sarah?" Charles inquired.

"No," Ricardo responded, "I just wanted to take care of her. It was only later that I discovered she had been dating my brother."

Charles's eyes widened in surprise. "Jeez, you mean the one who got shot?"

"Yes," Ricardo confirmed, "We only pieced it together recently."

"Quite the coincidence," Charles remarked. "Alright, I gotta run. I'll give you a call later."

Sarah continued down the hallway but came to another locked door. Fueled by a surge of adrenaline, she impulsively seized a nearby chair and launched it against one of the hallway windows. The impact was more powerful than expected, sending shards of glass flying as the window broke into many pieces. Hopefully no one heard. Cautiously, she peered out and still saw no one, so quietly extracted pieces of glass. As she worked, her stomach ached, and her heart beat fast. While removing glass shards, a sudden sharp pain sliced through her hand. Startled, she glanced down to discover a jagged piece of glass had cut into her skin. *Ouch! Damn! Blast!* Swearing softly to herself, she grabbed her flimsy scarf, wrapped it around the wound, and cleared the remaining remnants.

Gingerly, she eased herself onto the slanting roof, the dizzying height making her head spin slightly. Taking a deep breath to steady her nerves, she stretched out her right hand and grasped the vines. Her left hand reached out to balance her, but suddenly, the vine snapped. She swung violently against the wall, scraping both legs and biting back a cry of pain. With sweat threatening to make her fingers slip even more, she knew she had to move quickly. Mustering every ounce of courage, she carefully scrambled down, until she reached the garden below, her heart still beating hard from the adrenaline. Her knee throbbed, and blood oozed from the scrapes on her legs, but she found the strength to run. She climbed over a fence and fell to the ground on the other side. She jumped up and sprinted to a group of trees, then gulped for breath as she wondered which direction to go in. She often got lost in a mall, never mind a forest!

Immersed in a conversation with a fellow agent, Charles was abruptly jolted from the exchange by the unmistakable sound of gunfire. Without a moment's hesitation, both agents instinctively dropped to the ground, swiftly drawing their weapons. The urgency heightened when a voice pierced the chaotic scene: "Man down!" A Federale's cry pierced the air.

Reacting swiftly, Charles and his fellow agent cautiously maneuvered around the shelter of a squad car, only to be met with the harrowing sight of Ricardo on the ground, blood seeping from a grievous wound.

"Get this man to a hospital, quickly!" Charles bellowed urgently, his authoritative voice cutting through the tense atmosphere.

Agent Williams, scanning the surroundings, yelled, "There's the gunman! He just drove off in that white SUV."

"That's Harry Whelan's," Charles exclaimed with frustration. "Damn him to hell." In a heartbeat, he jumped into his car and followed the trail of the speeding jeep. Charles was unfamiliar with the terrain, and the chase was leading him up the mountain. Conscious of the drop below him and the loose boulders scattered on the road ahead, he tried to keep his jeep steady. He struggled to keep from slipping off the narrow, winding road. He called for backup. A bad signal made it impossible to give clear directions, but he knew they could track his whereabouts from his phone. He looked up, and the SUV was no longer in his sight. Charles' foot was flat to the pedal. His cell phone rang. Through the static, he heard Harry's voice and said, "Why don't you give up, Harry? I won't stop 'til I catch up with you." Driving with one hand proved even more dangerous.

Laughing like a maniac, Harry said, "Oh, I'm not sure about that. You had better look for your little girlfriend. She's in the abandoned villa behind the hotel, and I gave instructions to Pedro to get rid of her if he didn't hear from me by one p.m."

Charles's blood pressure peaked. He felt dizzy and nauseous. *Did I hear right? Did Harry really take Sarah prisoner?* His watch showed twelve forty. He screeched to a stop and recklessly reversed back down the road, hoping no other cars would hinder his careless driving. He found a small opening, enough to be able to turn around, and raced back down the mountain with the fury of a madman.

Charles thought, Damn that Harry. If anything happens to her, I'll kill him with my bare hands.

15

Charles stopped a little way down the road. He hid by some trees outside the old, deserted villa, then called for back-up. As usual, he didn't have the patience to wait, so he crept like a panther and scrambled over the wall and into the gardens. Pedro was enjoying his cigarette, so didn't notice the stealthy figure that crept into the main house. Once inside, Charles checked the ground floor. No sign of Sarah. He saw a door to the basement and tried the handle. It was locked. The heavy metal made it impossible for Charles to break it open. He whispered Sarah's name. No response. He quietly approached Pedro from behind and put a gun to his head.

"Where is Sarah?" he demanded, "And no tricks. Your pal Harry's going to jail for attempted murder, so you had better cooperate."

It didn't take much to convince Pedro. He took Charles straight to the basement and unlocked the door where Sarah had been imprisoned. They both peered into the empty room.

"She's gone," exclaimed Pedro with a mixture of disbelief and awe, his gaze fixed upon the wooden door. He flinched when Charles cuffed him. They were joined by a couple of officers; one took Pedro to the squad car while the other joined Charles to search the rest of the house.

Pedro was not lying. Sarah was gone. "Bloody hell," said Charles, "I guess she really did escape. A real Miss McGuyver. Question is, where did she go?"

The Mexican officer looked at him, puzzled. "Mac?"

"Never mind," said Charles. "Make sure you search the surrounding area; she might be lost or even hurt. Contact me immediately if you find anything."

He hoped that wherever she was, she was safe. Charles drove down to Santa Maria Hospital to check on Ricardo, who was still in surgery. He sat on the uncomfortable plastic chair next to Agent Williams. "You can go for a break. I'll keep watch," he told the agent.

"Thanks. Can I get you something?"

"Black coffee, strong and hot," said Charles.

Charles's worry for Sarah consumed him as he waited. He couldn't shake the feeling of guilt for not expressing his feelings to her. He knew he had to find her and let her know how he felt, no matter the circumstances. To ease the tension, his mind replayed all the moments they had spent together, which made him realize how much he cared for Sarah.

After a short hike, Sarah recognized the territory. She reached the hotel breathless, hot, and extremely thirsty. The temperature was unusually high. She stopped at the door and calmed herself down.

Sarah's return to the hotel was a mix of relief and embarrassment. She had been through quite an ordeal, and her appearance showed it. The concierge's puzzled look only added to her unease.

With a quick glance in the mirror, she sneaked past reception to avoid any further attention and hurried to her room. Her priority was to get cleaned up and rehydrated.

After a quick shower, she rushed around the room, gathered her belongings, and threw them into a suitcase. The cork from the wine bottle from her first date with Charles was on the dresser. She dropped it in the waste basket, thought about it, then retrieved it a moment later and threw it in the suitcase.

So, if Harry was the English guy that Ricardo mentioned, that meant both Charles and Ricardo had been telling her the truth. She felt guilty about not believing Ricardo and wondered whether Charles genuinely cared for her or was just using her. She liked him a lot, but right now, she was angry with him. He should have been around to protect her from that madman Harry.

She went down to reception and paid the hotel bill and waited for the taxi to the airport. Even if Harry or Pedro showed up, there were too many people around for them to chance anything. There was only one flight, and she was getting on it no matter what, even if a bit of *la mordida* had to be used. She wrote Charles a quick note. He had lied to her, put her in danger, and he was married. It was best just to leave without any emotional goodbyes. After John, she didn't need any more heartaches. A few tears dropped on the hotel stationery as she slid it into the envelope. She gave it to the reservation clerk with a twenty-dollar bill for assurance of its delivery.

Sarah's nerves were on edge as she waited for her flight at the airport. The delay only added to her frustration and anxiety. She sought refuge in a strong coffee with a generous pour of Baileys, hoping it would help calm her nerves. Her eyes darted around the busy airport, and she couldn't shake the feeling that she was being watched or followed.

She pulled out her novel and pretended to read. When a

stranger approached her, trying to strike up a conversation, Sarah's reaction was irritation. She was in no mood for small talk, and her focus was on staying alert and aware of her surroundings. "I'm busy; go away," she snapped at the stranger.

He gave her a strange look and sat far away from her. As the minutes ticked by slowly, Sarah felt like she was trapped in a suspenseful thriller. She was eager to board the plane and put some distance between herself and the troubles she had encountered in Mexico.

16

In the hospital waiting area, Charles sat anxiously in the stiff plastic chair, his gaze fixed on the closed door leading to the room where Ricardo was having surgery. The sterile smell of disinfectant aggravated his nose. He looked around the bustling emergency room. He heard the muffled conversations from people seeking medical attention or waiting for loved ones. He saw the worried looks on their faces, each carrying their own stories of pain. Charles fidgeted, his fingers tapping nervously against the armrest, and the rhythmic ticking of a wall clock irritated him as the passing seconds felt like an eternity. The harsh fluorescent lights overhead hurt his tired eyes. Charles hated hospitals; the memories of his childhood flooded his mind. He was only twelve when his mother had been diagnosed with cancer and had spent many hours in and out of them before she recovered. She survived the next ten years before the cancer returned and took her life. He never mentioned that to Sarah. It was a stark reminder that death could manifest unexpectedly, at anytime, on anyone.

Agent Williams brought him a coffee, and they sat in silence. Charles was tormented by the thought that the bullet that hit Ricardo might have been meant for him. After Sarah had told Charles her story, he had met with Ricardo. They had even shared a laugh at the misconception of each other being the enemy. The partnership between Ricardo and Charles had taken an unexpected turn with the revelation that Harry was the Englishman and involved in the criminal activities they were investigating. Despite their initial differences and suspicions, Ricardo and Charles were optimistic their combined skills and knowledge would lead to the dissolving of this criminal network. Ricardo was driven by the desire for closure and revenge for his brother's death, while Charles was eager to complete this assignment and return home. Another half hour passed until the doctor emerged from the ER. "*Signor* Castillo has made it through surgery, but we won't know anything until he awakes. He is recuperating in room 207."

Charles and the agent parked themselves outside the room, and the silence continued.

Agent Williams spoke first. "How did you know Harry was your guy?"

"I'd been in touch with my contact in the FBI. She had been comparing FBI and DEA files and found the connection, which led her to believe Harry was the ringleader and was working closely with *Don* Manuel Gonzalez. She came to visit me in Mexico to discuss her findings, but we were still unsure."

The conversation reminded Charles of the encounter with Sylvia and how Sarah had thought they were romantically involved. As soon as Ricardo was out of surgery, Charles would have to find Sarah and explain everything to her. He hadn't heard from his agent about Sarah's whereabouts. He hoped she was swilling in a foamy bath and resting. The day had been a whirlwind, and he knew she deserved a break after everything they'd been through. However, Sarah was not answering her phone or her mobile. *Had she lost it?* He glanced at the clock every few minutes. The longer he went without news, the more his worry grew. But he couldn't leave until he heard news about Ricardo.

The sudden and alarming beeping noise brought Charles back to the present. The medical staff rushed to Ricardo's room. Through the window of room 207, Charles and Agent Williams anxiously watched as doctors desperately tried to revive Ricardo. A nurse yelled, "BP's dropping. He's going into V-fib."

The doctor yelled orders. The defibrillator's electric shocks pulsed through Ricardo's body, but despite the efforts, the situation appeared dire. After what felt like an eternity, the only sounds that filled the room were the steady beeps and blips of the monitors diligently tracking Ricardo's vital signs. He had survived. The two agents breathed a sigh of relief. Charles, still in shock over what just happened, rubbed his aching head. "I need to contact a family member, so I need to get back to the office."

Agent Williams nodded. "I'll stay here until someone arrives."

"Thanks," said Charles. Just then, his mobile rang. It was Agent Johnson.

"I just informed Ricardo's maid about his situation. She told me the girl Carmen was with her."

"I'm going there now," said Charles.

He sped to Ricardo's ranch to find a hysterical *Senora* Guevera, Manuel's maid, and a teary-eyed Carmen. The truth about *Don* Manuel was a blow to *Senora* Guevera. She had never questioned anything about her employer. The two women hugged each other as the sobbing increased. When Carmen calmed down, Charles asked her if she had known about Manuel's business.

"I knew my Godfather was involved in drugs, but I thought only in a small way. He was always so good to me. But how is Ricardo? He is the only one I have to take care of me."

"He's tough. He will be okay."

"I need to go and see his mother. She has a weak heart, so I don't know how she will handle this." said Carmen.

Charles told her to sit down as he needed to ask a few questions before she left. "Do you know anything about the stolen drugs Sarah supposedly saw in my hotel room?"

Carmen wiped her eyes. "Papa asked me about it, and I lied, but he would believe anything I told him."

"So, you did steal the drugs?" Charles insisted.

"Yes, I am so sorry. I wanted to make Sarah suspicious of you, so she would leave Mexico. I was jealous of her. I thought Ricardo was paying too much attention to her.

I—."

Charles interrupted her and thought about the conversation he had had with Ricardo.

"There was nothing between Sarah and Ricardo. He was just a good friend." Charles shook his head. "Where is Sarah now?"

"I don't know. She must have gone to her hotel."

"Okay, I'll get someone to take you to Ricardo's mother's house and then to the hospital."

Charles had not slept, but his adrenaline kept him going. It was time to find Sarah and explain the situation. He called for an agent to pick up the ladies, and he made his way to his car. He drove quickly back to the hotel. The lobby was quiet, with only a few guests milling about. He approached the front desk, where the receptionist gave him a polite smile.

"Excuse me," he said, trying to keep his voice calm. "I'm looking for a guest, Sarah Houghton. Have you seen her recently?"

The receptionist frowned slightly and shook her head. "I'm sorry, sir. I haven't seen her. But let me check." He typed on the keyboard. "Sir, apparently she has checked out. Are you Charles Benson?"

"Yes."

"She left a note here for you."

The clerk handed him the envelope. Charles thanked him and sat in a secluded corner of the lobby and read the note.

Charles:

I am writing this letter with a heavy heart and a deep sense of anger. I made the decision to leave without saying goodbye. There was only one flight home, and I felt it was the safest choice for me at the time. I want to express that I now realize I was wrong about both you and Ricardo being involved in the drug dealing, and I sincerely hope you can apprehend the real culprit, Harry. I've had my fill of danger, and it's an experience I never want to repeat.

My emotions are mixed, Charles. On one hand, I am upset about feeling deceived and possibly used as your cover, and I've also learned that you are married. I don't know the full circumstances, but I feel so angry and cannot be involved with a married man. So, let's part ways with the memories we shared. We had some enjoyable times together, and I won't forget them, but I must move forward with my life.

My comfort zone is back in Los Angeles, where I plan to continue my life. I wish you all the best in your endeavors.

Take Care,
Sarah.

Charles choked up as he put the letter in his jacket pocket. He felt confused. Should he leave it alone or try and explain to

Sarah how he felt? He decided on the latter and climbed back in his car and raced to the airport, hoping he was not too late. He threw his keys to a valet, then ran through the terminal and through security. A customs officer yelled, "Sir, you need to stop there!"

Charles flashed his badge and said it was a matter of international security. The confused office allowed him through.

Sarah heard the announcement for the boarding of her flight. She groaned at the thought of the very last seat in the very last row of the small Boeing 737. Normally, she was one of the last passengers to board. There was nothing worse than sitting on a stuffy plane. But not this time. Today, she none too politely, pushed her way through the crowd to find her seat. She would feel safer sitting on the plane.

Charles headed toward the jetway, but the ticket agent refused him entry. He showed his badge to her and tried to use his charm, but she didn't budge with her decision. Security had called ahead to warn them. He looked through the window and watched the plane taxi to the runway. He slammed the window and slumped down, afraid he may never see her again. He trudged back to his car, each step laden with the weight of an indescribable ache in his chest. The air around him seemed thicker. He could hardly breathe. He walked slowly, regaining momentum, as he thought about her on the way to his car.

Back at the office, Charles focused his energy on his paperwork. He was determined to fulfill his obligation to track down Harry Whelan. That's the least he could do. Sarah's escape meant Harry had no leverage, but where was he? It was so easy to make oneself disappear in this country.

16

Due to the success of the raid, MI6 had issued a recall summoning him back to the UK, so he would be leaving Mexico the following day. Although this meant that the responsibility for resolving the situation with Harry Whelan now rested in the hands of the local police, he would still keep himself in the loop.

17

'The strong hands on her shoulder jolted her; a sensuous feeling rippled through her body. It was him. He had tracked her down. She was impressed. As he massaged her body gently, he told her he was now divorced, and they could be together forever.

She smiled at him and said, "I can't believe it. I always tried to imagine what it would be like, what you would say, what I would say, and all I can say is, let's go!"

She slowly arose, their eyes locked. They walked out the door hand in hand, happy they were united again. They both knew they had a future together as they silently strolled along the boardwalk'.

Sarah closed the book she had been reading in Mexico, as she sat in her cozy living room in her Long Beach condo, a world away from the tumultuous events of her time spent there. It seemed like happy endings were elusive for her, and the memories of her time in Mexico, both the thrilling and the painful, still lingered in her mind.

Two months had passed since she returned to California. One day, she saw a news report on CNN about the drug bust, which also hinted at that a child trafficking ring was also involved. Ricardo and Charles had never mentioned that part, thought Sarah. It also mentioned that one of the agents had been shot. She had no means to contact anyone to see who it was. Maybe she could call the DEA or FBI, but she doubted whether she could find a number for either of them, let alone get information. She hoped it wasn't Ricardo, as he had had too many tragedies in his life already.

As she sat in her peaceful surroundings, Sarah couldn't help but wonder if there would ever be a true happy ending to her own story. Her thoughts moved on to Charles. How could she have such strong feelings for him in such a short time? It was unlike her. She thought that she would never get over losing John. But there was something special about Charles. However, she realized he had just been using her as a cover. Damn him. Was he back in England with his family? She sometimes wondered if he would look her up. It wouldn't have been hard to track her down. Did she want him to? Her heart said yes; her head said no.

Sarah loved living in Belmont Shores, which was a popular spot in Long Beach, California. Her travel agency was nestled in between a funky clothing shop and a trendy bar. Her business, despite the changing times and the convenience of the internet, still thrived. She catered to a specific clientele, the older and more affluent crowd who appreciated the personal touch and the convenience of having all their travel arrangements meticulously handled.

Her cozy condo was ideally situated, just a street away from the beautiful beach, offering her the soothing sound of waves whenever she needed a moment of tranquility. Her daily routine was comfortable, with her agency's office just four blocks away. As most of her clients preferred in-person meetings at the office, she rarely needed her car except for those occasional business meetings in various parts of bustling Los Angeles.

Today, she needed to get some fresh air, so walked two blocks to her favorite coffee bar, Beans and Has-beans, who made the best lattes in town. She entered and paused for a moment, taking in the aroma from freshly cooked muffins and strong Columbian coffee. She much preferred this place to somewhere like Starbucks.

"You're early today," said Mark, the barista.

"Yes, I'm playing hooky."

At this hour, the regulars hadn't arrived. It was a place where unknown celebrities hung out, struggling actors or those who had had the chance of fame and lost it for whatever reason. Most of the employees here had a script in their 'back pocket'... just in case. The seats were comfortable, and management didn't mind how long a patron would hang out, even if they made one coffee last two hours.

Sarah ordered a latte and a blueberry scone. She called the office. "Anne, I've decided to take the rest of the day off. I'll see you Monday."

"No problem," said Anne. "I just have a couple of things to finish, and I'll be leaving too. Have a great weekend." Anne was her reliable assistant and a hard worker but also a lot of fun.

Sarah finished her coffee and took a walk to the park. She sat on a bench and took in the beauty of the surroundings. It was almost the end of October, and flowers were still blooming, pink and purple impatiens, and fuchsia with white flowers. This was why she loved California. Most states back east were shoveling snow by now or battling high winds and torrential rain. As her mind drifted towards Mexico, a flood of memories engulfed her, vivid and haunting. Countless nights had been spent grappling with the relentless echoes of trauma, each replay diving deeper into the recesses of her consciousness. The memory of that kidnapping seeped into her dreams, waking her up many times through the night as she relived the scenes. In hindsight, she acknowledged the sheer luck that had allowed her to escape from that perilous situation, alive.

Her thoughts were disturbed when she witnessed a distressing scene unfold before her. A woman, probably late thirties, shabbily dressed, was yelling at a young girl. The woman's aggression towards the young girl tugged at Sarah's compassionate nature. She hesitated for a moment, contemplating whether to intervene. The woman looked like she was about to hit the child, but abruptly changed her mind when she saw Sarah, so hurried away. Sarah covered her nose as the stench of body odor, cheap cigarettes, and alcohol wafted from the woman as she passed by her. The young girl shuffled down the path a few yards behind the woman, sniffling and begging her to slow down. She stopped short when she saw Sarah.

Sarah looked at the young girl. "Are you okay?"

The girl looked up with her big brown eyes and shook her head. Sarah handed her a tissue. The girl hesitated at first but then grabbed it and wiped back the tears.

"What's your name?" asked Sarah.

"I'm not supposed to talk to strangers."

"Good point. If I tell you my name and you tell me yours, then we won't be strangers anymore, will we?"

The girl looked into Sarah's face with a thoughtful stare. She stopped crying, blew her nose, and said, "Olivia."

"My name is Sarah."

"That's a nice name."

"Thank you. Yours is a beautiful name and very unusual."

"You think so?" said Olivia as she threw her long, tangled

locks behind her. Sarah imagined what she would look like after a hot bath and shampooed hair.

"Yes, Olivia, I do. Was that your mother who passed by me a few minutes ago?"

"Yes. It's okay. She won't leave me. She'll be back later."

"Where do you live?"

"In an apartment just past the park," she said and pointed to a cluster of trees.

Sarah bit her lip and took a deep breath. She knew the area Olivia was referring to, and although it wasn't quite Skid Row, it was a close second.

"It's my birthday today, and mother promised to take me out to McDonalds, but she forgot."

"Oh, I'm so sorry to hear that. So, how old are you, Olivia?"

"I'm eleven."

Sarah was surprised. Looking at her petite frame, she looked younger, but Sarah realized through this brief conversation how street-smart she was. "Well, how about if you stay here, and I will go to that diner over there and bring you a hamburger?"

Sarah knew that hunger would take precedence over her reluctance to stay put.

"I, er..." Olivia hesitated. "I don't know if I should."

"Okay, last chance," insisted Sarah.

"Okay, I'll wait here."

In the diner, Sarah ordered a hamburger with fries and an orange juice, knowing she would have to convince Olivia that it would do her more good than a soda. She was served quickly and hurried back to the park. They sat on a bench while Sarah drank her milkshake, and Olivia ate ravenously. As she finished the last drop of orange juice, she looked at Sarah sheepishly.

"Did you buy dessert?"

Sarah laughed. "Of course." Sarah couldn't help but smile as Olivia delved into the chocolate pudding with enthusiasm, spilling a little on her grubby blouse. At the same time, Sarah's throat ached with sorrow.

In between bites, Olivia said, "You talk funny."

"Blame it on the English accent."

"You mean English from England?"

"Yes. Have you ever been to England?"

"I've never been nowhere."

"Anywhere!"

"Huh?"

Sarah always corrected people's bad English. "Never mind."

Olivia finished every crumb but didn't move. The park was getting busy, and their bench was shared by an elderly gentleman who nodded his head in acknowledgment then continued to read his newspaper.

"So, tell me again why you speak funny?" asked Olivia.

"Well, I wouldn't say funny. How about different? I'm originally from England. It's like if you are from California, then you speak differently to someone who maybe lives in Alabama."

"How do they talk in Alabama?"

Sarah put on her best Southern accent, and Olivia burst out laughing.

"That's even funnier than your accent."

"Well, it might not be totally accurate."

Olivia continued to laugh. She then slurped the last drops of juice and walked to the trash can to deposit the empty bag and cup. Sarah was pleased that she didn't throw the garbage on the ground.

"I think it's time you should be going home."

"Can we please stay a little longer?" pleaded Olivia.

"Okay," replied Sarah.

The gentleman left, and Olivia lay next to Sarah as the sun slowly disappeared behind the horizon. Sarah wondered if Olivia's mother would show up. Olivia had fallen asleep with her head on Sarah's shoulder until she gently woke her. "Olivia, it's late, and I don't see anyone in the park. Do you know where your mother could be?"

"Probably drunk," said a sleepy Olivia. She hangs out with her boyfriend who lives close by. She's probably passed out again."

It was said in such a matter-of-fact tone, as if it were normal. Sarah's sympathy grew exponentially. She wanted to take this young child in her arms and give her a tight hug.

"Don't worry," continued Olivia, sitting up. "I know where they could be, and if I don't find them, I have my own key for the apartment. Thanks for dinner."

"Will I see you again?" asked Sarah.

"Maybe. I hope so." She smiled and took off.

Waiting until Olivia was out of sight, Sarah slowly walked back to her condo. The encounter served as a poignant reminder of her recent decision to become a foster mom. She had registered at the local social services office for their upcoming foster parent orientation session. It would be a good chance to make a positive impact on a child's life.

She tried to imagine what it would be like to have a child in her care. *Would she make a good mother?* She put the key in the lock and opened the front door. *Should she get another dog or cat?* In her younger years, she always had her furry companions. However, due to her frequent travels, finding someone reliable to care for them became a challenge. Additionally, she was hesitant to entrust her animals to conventional animal care facilities.

As these thoughts swirled in her mind, a sense of loneliness crept in, though she remained steadfast in her decision not to settle down with a man just yet. She sat on her sofa with a glass of wine and then another, but sleep was evading her. The young girl brought back memories of Mexico. If the same people had also been involved in child trafficking, she hoped that the authorities were able to disband the organization. However, she knew that the intervention would only make a temporary pause in the cycle of such atrocities. Somewhere else in the world, these horrendous deeds would likely be carried on by someone else; a grim reality that seemed relentless and unyielding.

She thought about Olivia and her living situation. *Should I report this blatant neglect to the police or child services? I should call my friend Alan? He always has good advice.* Sarah pondered about her own childhood. She was lucky to have had such lovely foster parents. They had been so kind and had taught her a lot.

18

"Daddy, daddy! You're home."

Charles was almost knocked over when his two children, Charles Jr. and Meghan, ran into his arms. They hugged him hard and then began the usual routine, smothering him with hugs and kisses.

"Where have you been? How long are you staying? Will you take us to the park?"

His wife Jane smiled. "Come on, children. Let daddy relax a bit, and then he can give you all the attention you need."

She ushered the children out of the room then kissed Charles gently on the cheek. Charles and Jane had been married straight out of university but after twenty years had grown apart. They still cared for each other but just as friends and parents of their children. The divorce wasn't final, and although the occasion arose many times to have extra-marital affairs, Charles had never been unfaithful to his wife, until he had met Sarah.

"How are you, darling?" asked Jane.

Charles admired her good looks, with a little blush to highlight her cheekbones and lipstick to accentuate her full lips. She always looked fresh and natural.

"Good. Tired," he replied wearily. "This last assignment took its toll. I'm starting to wonder if I'm getting too old for this. Perhaps it's time for a change."

"Like what?" Jane inquired, "You thrive on this kind of work, but it's tough for a spouse or partner. The constant fear of a knock on the door, dreading news of your demise. That is probably the main reason you and I split up."

Charles gazed at her affectionately, nodding his head, acknowledging the truth in her words. Perhaps, in another lifetime, they might still be together, or perhaps not. Charles thought that this was a good opportunity to discuss the move to the States with her.

"Jane, I was wondering. What would you think about if I decided to move to the States? The children are old enough to come over for holidays. Or maybe you could consider moving there too?"

"Darling, that would probably be a good move for you. Regarding the rest of us moving, I would have to discuss it with the children. But right now, they are both in a good place. They are involved in lots of activities, have great friends, and are doing well academically."

"You could easily get work with your qualifications as a pediatrician," said Charles.

She made coffee and sat next to Charles on the sofa. "Let's wait and see. However, we need to get the divorce finalized."

Charles looked at her. "Honey, if you are sure about a divorce, that's fine by me. Just know, I will always be there for you and the kids."

"We've had a good run together. Also," she hesitated, "I've met someone, and we are serious about each other. The kids like him too."

Charles' eyes widened. At first, he felt a little jealous, but then he thought about Sarah. He imagined the scent of her hair, the feel of her lips, and her enchanting smile. He had thought of her often over the past months and wondered how she was doing. Did she ever think about him? He wanted to see her again, but would he be welcome? But then he thought of his children liking another man and maybe calling him dad, which gave him a strange feeling.

"So, who is he, and where did you meet him?"

"Charles, you sound jealous."

"No, I would just feel a little weird if my children started calling him dad."

"Well, let's not get ahead of ourselves. We are not getting married—yet."

"Where did you meet him?" insisted Charles.

Jane blushed and said, "On the Internet."

"Oh, I see. To be honest, I've met someone too, but not sure if it will develop into something serious. I'll let you know if it does."

They both let out a sigh of relief and hugged each other tightly until Charles Jr. came running into the room and tackled Charles, then rolled on the floor with him. He loved his children dearly. They spent a pleasant evening together enjoying a home-cooked dinner. He tucked his children into bed, kissed Jane goodbye, and returned to the office.

The fact that Jane had accepted his possible move to the United States was a positive step, and he was hopeful that this change would bring new opportunities and happiness for both of them. The office was quiet, and the soft glow of his computer screen illuminated his expression. He had had no luck finding Harry, who had disappeared from the face of the earth. The Federales said that they would inform him if they found out any more information about his whereabouts.

18

Despite knowing Sarah's current residence, he decided not to reach out to her until he had firmly established himself in his new surroundings. The process of his transfer would take some time, and initially, he would be engaged on a consultant basis until he decided if he needed or wanted a change in his career.

Charles continued to reflect on his complicated history with Harry. Their relationship had always been strained, marked by Harry's jealousy and reckless behavior, but he couldn't help wondering about the extent of Harry's criminal activities. Charles hadn't seen him for the last few years and was a little surprised when he had showed up in Mexico. Charles wasn't the type to believe much in coincidences but had kept his suspicions to himself. The thought of bringing him to justice for the sake of Sarah's safety and his own peace of mind weighed heavily on him. His frustration with Harry deepened because he had callously informed Sarah that he was still married, hoping to destroy their relationship.

19

Sarah's decision to work on Sundays had been a deliberate choice, a sanctuary for her paperwork and thoughts. However, today was unlike any other. Concentration eluded her as her mind continually drifted to Olivia. The moments they had shared in the park lingered in her thoughts, leaving her emotionally stirred. Olivia possessed a wisdom far beyond her years, a result, no doubt, of the challenging circumstances that surrounded her.

The phone interrupted Sarah's thoughts. It didn't usually ring on Sundays, so she knew it would be her friend Alan. "Hello, Alan. Yes, I knew it would be you," she laughed. "I was thinking about you just last night. Sure, we can meet in an hour at the usual place."

Alan Hunter had been a close friend for nearly a year, and Sarah cherished their companionship. However, beneath their friendship, she sensed his unspoken desire for something more—something she couldn't reciprocate. She knew that when she told him about what happened in the park yesterday, he would find it fascinating. As a scriptwriter, he would see it as perfect material for a story. Sarah locked the office and made a detour to the park on her way to the coffee shop. She walked around the perimeter, but there was no sign of Olivia.

Disappointed, she continued her way to meet Alan.

The coffee bar was full of patrons sitting glued behind their laptops. Sarah was never sure what could occupy these college kids to spend hours staring at the screen. Surely it wasn't all homework. Alan waved and flashed Sarah his wide smile, revealing perfect teeth that stood out against his olive skin. She always suspected he was half-Italian, though he adamantly denied it.

"How are you?" he asked. "I got you a latte and your favorite poppy seed muffin."

"Thanks," said Sarah, sitting down.

"What's going on? It sounded like you needed someone to talk to."

Sarah chuckled, unable to suppress her amusement. "Are you a mind reader?" Alan had an uncanny knack for understanding her thoughts and emotions, except when it came to his own place in her heart. He was unlike most men she had encountered, refreshingly direct with no pretense. He spoke his mind, often without considering the consequences. Sarah vividly remembered the evening he had escorted her to a prestigious banquet. As one of the recipients walked on stage, Alan had leaned over to Sarah and said a bit too loudly, "Honestly, I can't fathom how this guy got that award. Total jerk." To their dismay, they soon realized they were seated next to the very committee responsible for selecting the award recipient, so needless to say, they left before the socializing began.

Sarah told him about the incident in the park.

"I know it's unfortunate, Sarah, but you can't save everyone. You used to rescue cats and dogs, and now snotty-nosed kids."

Sarah laughed. "I know, but this little girl is so precious. There's something about her that I find intriguing. What do you suggest I do?"

"Well, first of all, get social services to visit them at their apartment to see how bad it really is."

"What do you mean?" asked Sarah.

"If her living situation is unsuitable or unsafe, child services might consider placing her with a foster parent. Didn't you mention you applied to be a foster mother?" Alan inquired.

"Yes, but the process is moving slowly."

Alan pressed on, "Social services could find Olivia a temporary home until a permanent one becomes available. You wouldn't want her to end up in the system, moving from one foster home to another."

"Oh, God forbid," said Sarah. "I guess not everyone is as lucky as I was finding great foster parents. A friend of mine grew up in foster care and did not have a happy childhood."

"Just think about it carefully. Talk to that friend of yours who knows about this kind of thing." Alan assured Sarah that if she was meant to help Olivia, then it would happen. He was a great believer in letting the universe take its course.

The following week, Sarah visited the park several times, but to her chagrin, there was no sign of Olivia. She found herself thinking way too much about this kid. Laughing to herself, she thought about Alan's description. Olivia wasn't snotty-nosed.

"Do you think I'm becoming obsessed?" Sarah inquired, turning to her assistant, Anne.

Anne shrugged. "I'm no psychiatrist, but you do seem unusually fixated on this child. It's almost like a real-life *Little Orphan Annie* story, or perhaps more like *Oliver* with the name Olivia."

Sarah chuckled, familiar with Anne's tendency to reference movies. "You and your movie references."

19

It was Friday night. The week had passed painfully slowly. Business was quiet; not that Sarah worried as it had been a great year with good commissions.

"Anne, will you lock up for me? I feel like a walk."

"*A Walk in the Park,*" quipped Anne.

Sarah left the building laughing. She had known Anne for years and still found her silly references to movies funny. As she walked down the boulevard, she found herself once more at the park. It had been almost a month since she had sat on this very same bench where she had first met Olivia. She sat reading her novel on Kindle when a familiar voice interrupted her.

"What's that?"

"How about 'hello, how are you' before I answer that?" Sarah said, looking at Olivia, who stood by the bench with her arms folded, a smirk on her not-so-clean face.

"Hi."

"Well, hello to you, my young friend. Where have you been lately?"

"Here and there," answered Olivia. "Where have you been? I haven't seen you around."

"I guess our timing was off," said Sarah. "I've come by here many times."

"Looking for me?"

"What makes you say that?"

"I dunno. Just thought we were, like, friends."

"Could say that," said Sarah. "Are you hungry?"

"Always," replied Olivia.

Sarah winced, contemplating when this slender frame of a young girl had last enjoyed a decent meal or if wholesome nourishment had ever been a regular part of her life.

"Okay, wait here."

"Can I come with you?"

Sarah hesitated, "I don't want to be accused of kidnapping."

"Don't worry, the waitress in the diner knows me, and she'll think I've kidnapped *you.*"

As they walked across the park, a tender warmth enveloped Sarah when Olivia slipped her hand into hers. The simple act of intertwining fingers persisted until they reached the diner. Sarah couldn't help but feel deeply touched by this gesture, a connection that spoke volumes beyond words.

They settled in a booth, and the waitress approached them.

"Hello, Olivia. Who have you hoodwinked this time, to buy you food?"

The waitress smiled at Sarah. "I'm just joking, actually. I sometimes give her a sandwich when she hangs out by the door."

Sarah told Olivia to go to the bathroom and wash her hands.

"That's very kind of you," said Sarah, "Do you know her mother?"

The waitress nodded. "She's had a few handouts also. It's a sad situation. When her mother is sober, she's not a bad person, but the drugs are doing her in."

"I was thinking of calling social services," whispered Sarah before Olivia returned to the table.

"Maybe a good idea," said the waitress and left to put in the order of pancakes.

"What's a good idea?" asked Olivia, sitting down.

"Oh! to have an extra side of fruit," said Sarah quickly.

Sarah cringed a little when Olivia smothered the pancakes in too much syrup. "That's a lot of sugar, young lady."

"It makes me feel good and gives me energy."

Sarah sighed. "We'll need to discuss that sometime. We don't want you to become diabetic, do we? How would you like it if you had to stick a needle in your body every day?"

Olivia screwed up her face. "Yuk. I think my mother's boyfriend must be that, as I seen him with a needle. I can't watch. It makes me feel sick."

Sarah forced a smile. She doubted Olivia's mother's boyfriend was injecting insulin. They finished up with a vanilla ice cream, and then Sarah asked what Olivia was going to do today. She faltered before speaking. "Well... I, er... I'm not sure. I haven't seen my mother since yesterday, and she didn't look so good."

"Oh, my God, where have you been? Who's looking after you?"

"Shit! You ask a lot of questions."

"Please don't swear. I'm just concerned about you, that's all."

"Well, don't be. I can look after myself."

Sarah wished she could take her home, give her a bath and a decent bed for the night, but she knew it would be against the law. Reluctantly, Sarah let Olivia go. Not knowing exactly where she was going gave her an uneasy feeling. At that moment, there was nothing more she could do.

Returning to the comfort of her cozy condo, Sarah picked up the phone and dialed a familiar number. She felt guilty, recognizing that a small child was out there in the darkness, searching for a mother who didn't seem to care about her own daughter. "Hello, is that you, Elizabeth?"

Elizabeth, a longtime friend of Sarah's, immediately answered. "Yes, Sarah, you sound a bit off. What's going on?"

"Well, today in the park...." She explained everything that

had happened and asked who she should call. Elizabeth knew someone personally in child services and told Sarah she would give her friend a call first thing in the morning.

Sarah made her way to her desk and opened her laptop. She checked her application to social services and was pleased they had given her an interview that following Monday afternoon. As she was about to close her laptop, a spontaneous decision made her look through her collection of photos from her travels in Mexico. Each image brought a mix of emotions, some good, and some tinged with the bittersweet. As she examined the photos, a detail caught her eye—an image of herself she hadn't initially noticed, with a man lingering in the background. Peering closer, she was struck by a revelation: "Oh, my God, that's the guy who approached me about 'the package.'" Suddenly, the pieces fell into place, and she now understood the connection between that encounter and the mysterious incident with the falling rocks.

In that moment, she found herself wondering about Charles, envisioning him in the company of his wife and children, enjoying the warmth of a wonderful family time. She sighed, and with her glass of Cabernet in hand, she retreated into the comforting darkness of her bedroom, leaving behind the world's worries for a while. But, once again, sleep evaded her.

In the quiet solitude of her thoughts, Sarah found her mind entangled with a myriad of concerns. Charles and the enigmatic allure of Mexico, the unsettling presence of the elusive Harry Whelan, not having any knowledge of who got shot or whether they lived, and then there was Olivia—a current dilemma demanding her attention. The many thoughts rushing through her mind seemed to weave together, creating a tapestry of uncertainties, which followed her into her dreams.

The phone rang. Sarah picked it up. "Hi, Sarah, it's Elizabeth," came the voice on the other end of the line. "I've spoken to my friend in CPS. I asked her for information about your case, hypothetically speaking, if you know what I mean. I didn't want to alarm anyone until you have had a chance to find out a bit more about the kid's situation."

After a brief exchange with Elizabeth, Sarah gently hit end call, knowing that important decisions lay ahead. Sarah felt a mix of relief and anxiety. Today was her birthday. She found herself in a reflective mood, her thoughts drifting back to her own past, the places she had ventured, and the people who had crossed her path. Birthdays had a way of prompting introspection, making her question whether the right choices had been made along the way. Despite past financial missteps, she found herself in a comfortable position now. Her business thrived, she had the security of owning her home, and there was an employee she could wholeheartedly rely on. However, in the midst of this stability, the absence of a significant other became apparent.

Contemplating the prospect of a relationship, she couldn't ignore the complexities and problems that characterized her previous entanglements. Perhaps, she mused, being single was her destiny. That's why being a foster parent really appealed to her. The prospect of offering care and support to those in need would make her life seem worthwhile. With unwavering determination, she decided to prioritize the journey towards becoming a foster mom. She knew she needed to have a conversation with Olivia's mother and discuss possible arrangements for Olivia to have a healthier and more stable environment.

Another week went by before Sarah saw Olivia. She was sitting outside the deli, her face all forlorn. Despite the lingering warmth of November, Olivia appeared chilly in her thin trousers and blouse. Sarah walked slowly towards her. "Hi, stranger."

Olivia was reading a book. She looked up and smiled, "Hi."

"I'm going to get something to eat. Can I get you something?"

"You know me, never refuse food."

They sat inside, and when they had finished every bit of food served to them, Sarah said, "I have a present for you. A belated birthday gift."

Olivia's eyes widened. Sarah handed her a basic phone and said," I have programmed in my mobile number and the number for the local police. Did you want to add any school friends, maybe?"

"Why would I want a number for the police? I don't have any school friends. I haven't been to school forever. I hate school. The kids all laugh at me and my clothes."

Sarah saw tears welling up in her eyes. "I'm sorry, Olivia. Maybe I can help you."

Olivia wiped her eyes with the back of her hands and asked, "How?"

"First, we have to find your mother. I need to talk to her."

"Why?"

"Well, I am not your legal guardian, so I would need her permission if I was, let's say, to take you shopping."

"Okay," replied Olivia with a sigh.

"So, let's go look for your mother?"

Olivia looked down at the floor then back up at Sarah. Her brown eyes teared up a little once more. "Mmm... oh, okay. If we have to."

As they walked through the park. the sun shone in the clear

sky, and early morning joggers passed Sarah and Olivia at a steady pace. A few mothers played with their children. Olivia held Sarah's hand tightly. Sarah could sense that Olivia had a deep affection for her mother, considering all her mother's faults. It was only natural, but Sarah knew Olivia was tired of her present situation. "She must be worried about you. Maybe she's back at the apartment."

"Nah, she doesn't like being there. The people who hang out close by are scary. She feels safer in the park with her friends."

They wandered around for an hour but didn't find any trace of Olivia's mother. They were about to give up when Olivia spotted the usual crowd: friends of her mother.

"She's probably over there with those people."

"Okay, you stay here," insisted Sarah.

20

Sarah was conscious her breathing had become shallow and quick. Standing for a moment, she took some deep breaths and walked up to the table of the drinkers.

"Excuse me, may I ask a question?"

"Depends on who's asking," one of the men replied. He was a little less drunk than the others. The rest of the group chuckled at his smart comment.

As Sarah thought about Olivia, she found a renewed strength. "Do any of you know someone who might have a daughter called Olivia?"

"Is that little snot in trouble again?" slurred a woman slumped across the table, hanging onto an empty beer bottle.

Sarah recognized the wrinkled face and the same dirty clothing from the first time she had seen her. "Do you know her?" continued Sarah, knowing full well she was talking to the mother.

"Yup, that would be my shitty little brat." Once again, the crowd laughed. "Where is that stupid kid? I told her to wait for me."

"She did," said Sarah, biting her lip and holding back her anger. "I saw her by the diner, all alone."

"Well, I'm here, ain't I? Send her over."

"I will not. I need to talk to you."

Olivia's mother rose from the table but, too drunk to stand, fell to the ground. Another woman said, "Hey, lady. Give her some money, and the kid is yours."

The guys broke into laughter, and Sarah wished she was strong enough to knock them all off their smart asses. "Maybe I should just call the cops," said Sarah, pulling out her cell phone.

"Okay, lady. You better leave before you get hurt," said one of the men, standing up.

"I will come back in the morning. Tell that drunken bitch of a mother to be here at ten."

Sarah returned to Olivia. "I think it's best you just go home now. I told your mother I want to talk to her tomorrow and that she had better be sober. Can you make sure she gets over here?"

"Okay," said Olivia, "I'll see you tomorrow."

Sarah gave her a hug and waited until Olivia went in the direction of her home.

Sarah paced the apartment and practiced what she had to say to Olivia's mother. She wasn't even sure what she was going to say but knew she had to choose her words carefully. She would at least ask her permission to take Olivia shopping, as school was about to start.

Sarah envisioned the prospect of having someone like Olivia live with her. Her loneliness occasionally crept in, and the thought of companionship made Sarah feel good. She mulled over a recent conversation she had had with Alan. Was it true what he said? Was the reason her relationships never worked out because of what had happened with her own father? Could

Alan be right? He put it quite simply. "The first man in your life betrayed you. So how can you trust any other man?" Sarah didn't talk much about her past except with Alan. He did know her biological mother left her when she was only seven years old. Sarah was upset about that for a long time, until she discovered later in life her mother was suffering from mental problems due to her father's cruelty. Alan also knew about her adoptive parents. Alan had asked why her father had not kept her with him.

"Maybe because he went to jail."

"Oh, that's a good enough reason."

Sarah had continued, "He liked to drink. It was a mad dog he kept on a chain, but when it got loose, we all felt the consequences. Mom would tell me to go to my room."

She shivered as she thought about those nights. She didn't have to be told twice. By then, she'd become used to those drunken harangues, the midnight arguments he had had with Mom, and the sobbing that followed. She had assumed this was normal as she pulled the covers over her head to shut out the sounds. It was only later Sarah learned that kind of behavior could affect someone in adult life. The feeling of abandonment and resentment can be buried deep in the subconscious. Maybe that's why she was doubly upset about losing John. She thought that she had finally met her soul mate.

21

The following day, Sarah sat at her desk, eyeing the clock every few minutes.

"Anne, would you do me a favor?"

"Sure."

"Would you watch the office? I have an appointment at ten a.m."

"Okay. No problem."

Sarah grabbed her jacket and car keys and drove to the park and waited. A multitude of questions swirled in Sarah's mind, creating a web of uncertainties. *What if, despite the plans, Olivia's mother didn't show up? What if she objected to me accompanying Olivia on a shopping expedition? How would she react to the suggestion of rehabilitation? What if I threatened to call social services?*

Olivia's mother showed up twenty minutes late. Her unkempt hair hung in tangled strands over her face. She wore a worn, wrinkled dress that seemed to have seen better days, and it was paired with a moth-eaten sweater so damaged that even a charity shop would have turned it down. Sarah tried to stay calm. "Glad you could make it."

"I slept in. I'm tired and hungover. What do you want?"

"I want to know what you are going to do about Olivia. She

needs to be fed and clothed properly.

"How much you gonna give me?"

"What?" said Sarah.

"You heard. How much?"

"What do you mean, how much?"

"Well, it seems you're one of those lonely women who don't have kids," she sneered, letting out a scornful laugh. "Do you want to rent her for a few years?" She banged her hand on the table, still chuckling.

Sarah couldn't believe what she was hearing. She stared at this woman in disbelief and anger. "Are you on drugs or just completely insane?"

"Listen, bitch, I carried that kid for nine months and almost died, so she owes me. Her rich daddy took off, and I ain't got no money and no job. We live in a shit hole and eat from food banks."

Sarah couldn't help but think, *And buy drugs with government money.* "Look, I'm not buying your daughter. We have to go to CPS and fill out some paperwork and then appear before a judge so Olivia can be placed in foster care. Only until you have kicked the drug habit."

"What's CPS?"

"Child protection Services," replied Sarah, amazed at her ignorance.

"I ain't going to court."

Sarah's face reddened. "It's a straightforward process. I understand you've had some tough times, but by helping you, I will be helping Olivia. She's a good kid. I'll give you some money to help with therapy at one of the clinics. Maybe that can help you get back on your feet and find a job or something."

Olivia's mother opened her mouth to say something but

instead flopped onto the wooden bench and cried. Sarah offered her a Kleenex. The mother blew her nose and looked up. "My name is Mary Wilson. I was never married to Olivia's father. His family was wealthy." More tears rolled down her cheeks. "They tried to pay me off so I would leave him alone. They even suggested I have an abortion. But Richard, Olivia's dad, was rebellious and tried to prove he could live without his trust fund."

Sarah's voice softened. "So, what happened?"

"He was abusive with me, but when Olivia was born, he changed."

"Really? Olivia told me that she saw him beat you one day, so she kicked him."

"Yes, she did. She's got a lot of spirit, that kid. Funny, he didn't touch me after that."

"Then what happened?"

"He realized he couldn't live without his money. He had a heavy cocaine habit, so of course, he missed having money to buy it, so he left me to look after the kid."

"I'm so sorry," said Sarah. "But now you need to think of yourself and Olivia. You must stop drinking and whatever else you are doing."

"I ain't got no money. What am I supposed to do?"

Sarah offered a solution, "Well, I can give you a little and take you to Souls Harbor Mission. There, you can clean up, get some decent meals, and then ask them to help you get into rehab."

"What about Olivia?"

"She can stay with a foster family. I have actually applied to be one, so maybe when I'm approved, I can take her until you get back on your feet. However, you must come in to see a judge to sign a paper so we can get the process started."

Three long weeks later, two things happened. Sarah's application as foster mum was approved, and they got a day in court with the judge.

The initial hearing involved an appearance where the judge was informed about the circumstances leading to Olivia's need for foster care. The judge couldn't review any reports from social workers as no one had been involved with Olivia's case.

A week later, a subsequent court hearing was held in front of Sarah, Mary, and Olivia. Sarah, armed with a compelling case, eloquently presented her perspective to the judge. With Olivia's consent and Mary's supporting statement, Sarah was granted approval to become the foster mother.

After the court appearance, Sarah drove Mary downtown to the mission and discreetly handed some money to her. Olivia gave her mother a big hug and said a quiet goodbye, adding, "Please get better."

Mary Wilson watched as Sarah's car disappeared. A sly smile crossed her face as she made her way back to the park, tucking the cash securely into her bra.

Sarah drove back to her condo with an excited Olivia. She parked the car, and they walked in. They were both hungry, so Sarah heated up a frozen pizza. Olivia hadn't said much on the way back, so Sarah asked, "Are you okay, Olivia? You're very quiet."

Olivia looked up. "I am so excited. I dunno what to say. I just hope Mom will be okay."

"Don't worry, she's in a good place. They will help her get better."

"Does that mean I will have to go and live with her again?"

Sarah's throat tightened as she thought about the prospect of losing Olivia. Choosing her words carefully, she said, "Well, it depends on how your mom is doing. I mean, I can always come to visit, and you're more than welcome to stay on weekends. Don't worry; we'll figure out what's best for everyone."

Sarah took Olivia into the bathroom and filled the tub with warm water and bubble bath. With renewed energy, Olivia soaked and played with the bubbles. Sarah opened the door enough to hear Olivia singing 'Mean' by Taylor Swift. She sang with a surprisingly beautiful voice. Olivia noticed Sarah listening and stopped singing.

"Please don't stop. You have a beautiful voice."

"My mother didn't like me to sing."

"Well, guess what. I won't tell her. Okay?"

"Okay," said Olivia and continued singing.

After spending an hour in the soothing bath, Sarah led Olivia to the spare room and carefully dressed her in an over sized flannel shirt. They sat on the sofa drinking hot cocoa. An hour later Olivia was snugly settled in bed. Sarah pulled the blanket up to cover her fragile frame. Despite the daytime warmth in California, the nights could get chilly. Olivia closed her eyes and drifted into a deep slumber.

Sarah turned off the light, left the door open a little, and walked into the living room. She settled on the sofa and sipped on a glass of her favorite Merlot. Strangely, she didn't feel lonely anymore. The presence of Olivia in the next room brought a peacefulness and made the future look brighter. Even if she went back to live with her mother, Sarah would always be in her life.

After a restless sleep, a loud clatter awakened Sarah. The digital clock displayed 7 AM. Argh! She was not an early bird, especially on the weekends. She grabbed her bathrobe and staggered into the kitchen. Olivia handed her a cup, sporting a big grin.

"I couldn't find coffee, but I figured you were a tea drinker, coz you're English."

"Thank you, sweetheart," said Sarah as she sipped the drink. It took all her strength to keep it down. She smiled, hiding the distaste of the lukewarm beverage.

"It's probably not how you like it, but I've never made tea before."

"Don't worry," said Sarah. "I'll teach you."

In the kitchen, the small table was dressed haphazardly with table mats, napkins, and silverware, and Olivia proceeded to pour cereal into the bowls then passed the little milk jug to Sarah, spilling a few drops in the process. After breakfast, they cleared the table and washed the dishes. They sat down while Sarah drank a proper cup of tea, and the contented look on Olivia's face was apparent. She gave Sarah a breathtaking hug and said, "I am sooooo lucky. I want to be with you 'til I grow up and get rich and famous and can buy you a house and a boat and a Rolling Royce and pay for your nurse and…"

"Whoa," said Sarah, "Slow down." Sarah and Olivia laughed until it hurt.

They had one month before school started. "Okay, young lady, let's go. We have an errand to run."

Within twenty minutes, they arrived at Long Beach Mall. Sarah had never been particularly fond of malls. They tended to be noisy, and most of the stores carried the same generic items. She preferred the local mom-and-pop stores in Belmont Shores along the boulevard. However, the mall did offer a wider variety of children's clothing. The challenge, as always at the mall, was finding a parking spot. Sarah circled the block a couple of times, but no open spots appeared.

Olivia pointed out, "There's a parking garage."

Sarah hesitated. "I'd rather not park in there. It's quite expensive."

Olivia raised an eyebrow. "I thought you were rich."

Sarah chuckled. "I'm not rich, but I'm not poor either. I'm just careful with my money. Wait, there's a spot!"

She went to pull in when a Mercedes started to pull in from the other side of the street. There wasn't enough room for both of them, so they were unable to move either way. Sarah tried to wave the guy back, but he gave her the finger. Normally, this rude gesture didn't bother her, but this time, she didn't have the patience. She got out of her car and approached him. A white guy in an Armani suit, with perfect hair and skin, got out and yelled at her. "Listen, lady, I got here first.

"Honestly, you people who drive Mercedes think you own the bloody road."

Before the argument could continue, Olivia tugged at Sarah's skirt.

"Mom, Mom, I have to go to the bathroom... like, now."

Sarah took the lead. "Oh, honey, I'm sorry." She turned to the man and said,

"My poor daughter suffers from diverticulitis, and when she has to go, she has to go."

"Oh!" said the man when he saw Olivia. "I guess you win this time." He jumped back into his Mercedes and drove off, tires squealing.

Sarah parked the car and laughed. "I didn't know you were such a good actress, Olivia."

"Sometimes you just gotta do what you gotta do. What's diving cultis?" she asked.

I'll explain when we get home. We have more important things to do right now.

The noise was more deafening than usual. Sarah discovered there was a local talent competition going on when she saw the stage. They made their way through the crowd to watch children in sparkly costumes strut their stuff. Olivia was mesmerized.

"How would you like to take dance lessons?" Sarah asked.

"I dunno. I don't think I can dance. But I can sing."

"That's true. But you don't know how good you are at dancing until you take lessons. Maybe we can arrange some for you."

Olivia's eyes grew larger. Sarah also realized that this was all new to her as she hadn't even been in a mall before, something that most children took for granted.

They left the stage area as Olivia hummed and walked into a shop called Tots to Teens.

"Okay, girlfriend, start looking. See what appeals to you."

At first, Olivia just wandered around.

"Why don't you pick a few things so you can try them on?" asked Sarah.

"There's so much. I don't know where to start."

"Okay, then. What are your favorite colors?"

"Purple, orange, pink... I don't know. I've never thought about it."

"Which colors pop out to you?"

As she looked, Sarah suggested she begin with a pair of jeans. They picked a regular blue jean and a pair of navy corduroys. Sarah held onto them while they browsed through the tops. Olivia picked out four pretty T-shirts and two sweaters, one blue and one red. Sarah noticed Olivia gravitate to one of the

21

T-shirts. It was white with sparkles on a pattern of colorful butterflies. Sarah checked the price and, although it was twice as much as the others, she hoped Olivia would decide to buy it. Finally, a couple of pairs of pajamas. Olivia took her choices into the dressing room while Sarah browsed a few more racks, surprised at the price of kids' clothing. Olivia came out, did a little fashion show, and then chose two T-shirts, both sweaters, and the blue jeans.

"The other pants didn't fit."

"I'm surprised you didn't pick the white T-shirt. I thought you really liked it."

"I, er... well, it was a bit big for me."

"Okay, just leave the items in the dressing room. The sales assistant will take care of returning them to the correct racks," Sarah instructed.

As they waited by the cash register, another mother and daughter duo stood in line. The young girl wore a pout on her face. "I really want that white one, Mother," she said.

The assistant told the girl that it had been purchased and there were a couple of similar ones she could show her.

Sarah looked up and said, "Oh, if you're talking about the white T-shirt with all the sparkles, we didn't buy it. I think it's still in the dressing room."

"I feel hot. I'm going to sit outside," said Olivia.

"Okay," said Sarah.

The lady in front of Sarah told her to go ahead so they could go back and find the T-shirt. Sarah paid, but before she left the store, the assistant came to her. "Excuse me, ma'am. We still can't find that T-shirt. I found the tag in the dressing room. Are you sure your daughter didn't take it... er... by mistake?" she added.

Sarah reddened and said, "How dare you insinuate my child stole something? Check the racks; it probably got mixed in with some other clothes. And another thing, wouldn't it set off the alarm with those thingamajigs attached?"

"Actually, ma'am, the lower-priced items are not tagged with the sensors."

"Lower price? That T-shirt cost more than the other three together. Let me tell you, this will be the last time I or any of my family and friends will shop here." Sarah stormed out and looked for Olivia.

She wasn't on the bench. She was nowhere in sight.

22

Sarah's heart pounded. Where can Olivia be? Where would she go? Sarah combed the mall, checking every store. She approached a security guard and explained the situation. He immediately spoke into his radio, "Code Adam."

Sarah said, "What's happening?"

"Ma'am, whenever a child goes missing, we act on Code Adam, which means all doors exiting the mall will be guarded for one hour."

"Wow," said Sarah. She had never heard of this before. "So, what do I do?"

"Can you give me a description?"

Sarah showed him a photo on her mobile.

"Thank you," said the guard. "Please keep looking for her. Report back to me. Or after an hour if you don't find her." A concerned frown crossed his face. "We may have to call the authorities."

One hour felt like three to Sarah as she made her way back to the mall's security office. The sound of a familiar voice coming from the stage stopped Sarah abruptly. She pushed her way through the crowd, elbowing a couple of people, and ignored a woman who swore at her as she almost knocked the coffee out of her hand. Sarah gasped. There was Olivia, prancing back and forth on the raised platform like a superstar, wearing the stolen T-shirt, belting out 'Mean' by Taylor Swift. Sarah swore under her breath. She wanted to drag Olivia off the stage but thought it best to wait until she finished the song. As the audience applauded, Sarah rushed over to the back of the stage. Olivia was talking to a shabbily dressed boy about her own age.

Is this one of her street buddies? Has Olivia been fooling me all this time? As Sarah approached, the boy took off. Sarah shouted, "Olivia, don't you dare move." And she didn't.

Olivia looked at the ground. Sarah grabbed her arm, "Look at me. Why did you disappear like this? I thought you had been abducted."

"I... I knew you would be mad when you found out about the shirt."

"Mad? That isn't even close to what I feel. Humiliated, betrayed, angry, confused. Why did you steal it? You knew I was buying you some clothes."

"Well, I really liked this one, but it was expensive, and you said you were not rich... and I really wanted this, and..."

"Stop," said Sarah. "Yes, I said I was not rich, but I'm not poor. I'm just careful. I don't squander my money, but I love buying clothes for you. I've never had any children, and it felt good to treat you."

Olivia began to cry. "I'm sorry. I'm not used to people liking me... I... er...."

Sarah handed her a Kleenex. "Honey, I don't like you; I love you."

Olivia looked at Sarah with tears in her eyes. She hugged Sarah tightly as Sarah pushed back her own tears and gasped for breath from such a strong hug.

"Come on, let's go. I have to inform the guard I've found you.

By the way, why did you hang around?"

"I couldn't get out. The doors were, like, guarded by guys with guns. I think there was a bomb scare or something."

"That bomb scare was you. A lot happens when a child is reported missing."

"I'm sorry. Are you going to punish me?'

"Yes," said Sarah. "There are consequences when people do bad things, especially when they know they are wrong."

"I'm sorry. I don't want to end up like my mother and her friends."

Sarah swallowed hard. She almost returned the hug but knew she had to be firm.

"So, first, we're going to the bathroom so you can take off that shirt. We are returning it, and you will apologize to the ladies who work there. I have a good mind to return all these clothes, but I need you to look half decent when you go to school."

Sarah alerted security that Olivia had been found, then they marched back to the store in silence. Thankfully, there were no customers around. Olivia apologized to the manager. The manager turned to Sarah. "I certainly don't condone what the child did, but I do admire that she had the courage to come back and admit her mistake."

"Thank you, and I must apologize too," said Sarah. "I was wrong. I'm returning this shirt as a punishment to her, but I may sneak back and buy it another time."

On the way home, they were silent until Sarah said, "Olivia, when you were singing today, everyone stopped to listen to you. I felt very proud. You do have a lovely voice. However, now that you are living with me, you will have to prove that you can be trusted, and we will be setting up a schedule of chores before I arrange for any voice lessons."

"And dance lessons?' asked Olivia.

"Don't push your luck."

"I know you're not rich, but you ain't poor."

Sarah shook her head, hiding her amusement.

23

Charles stood holding a cardboard box and stared at what had been his office for most of his working life. He smiled at the cheap trophy atop his papers, which he had won when his MI6 cricket team beat MI5.

Fifteen years of lies, deceit, and pretense. He wasn't sure if he was doing the right thing moving to the States to do the same kind of work, but could he ever get used to a normal lifestyle? He had considered an offer with a high-end security firm but knew he would get bored quickly.

Jane and Charles had sat down with their children and had explained the situation to them. They were disappointed when they learned their parents would not be together as a couple, but were still excited about the chance to spend their holidays in California.

Jane flashed a secretive smile at Charles and whispered, "That would be a good break for me during the summer."

"I heard that, Mom. Do you want to get rid of us so soon?" teased Meghan.

"No, darling, I just—"

"I'm kidding," Meghan interrupted, enveloping her mom in a big hug. "It will be cool going to L.A. My friends will all be so jealous. There are so many things I want to do and see."

They all gathered around the dining table, enjoying a home-cooked dinner, and discussed excitedly the places they hoped to visit. Charles was happy to see them so excited. Amidst the cheerful chatter, his thoughts drifted to Sarah. Would she still have feelings for him? Was she possibly seeing someone else? He pushed aside these thoughts as he helped to clear up the dinner dishes. He kissed everyone goodnight and returned to the office.

He would be arriving in the US by the following week. His emotions vacillated between excitement and nerves as his thoughts drifted back to Sarah. She was owed an explanation about the situation and how it had changed, but he was unsure if she would even speak to him. He now understood her reluctance to let go of her emotions in Mexico after Ricardo had explained the situation with his brother, John.

As a non-US citizen, Charles could only be hired as an intelligence analyst with the FBI until his application to be a US citizen was approved. He had come highly recommended, and his fluency in Spanish was a plus. He chuckled to himself as when he was with Sarah, he pretended his Spanish wasn't that good.

Two weeks later, he was sitting in his new office. It was much bigger than his one back home. The FBI had more money to spend. Today marked the beginning of interactions with his new colleagues, a step toward adapting to the American way of life. Thankfully, his coworkers seemed enthusiastic about having a Brit on board, anticipating a touch of humor and cultural exchange. The prospect of friendly banter and camaraderie offered Charles a distraction from thinking about Sarah.

The FBI office was discreetly situated in a nondescript office building downtown, and Charles had temporarily rented a studio apartment close by until he decided on what area to live in... or what area he could afford to live in. Venice Beach, located on the west side of Los Angeles, was his first choice, a vibrant and eclectic neighborhood known for its distinctive character and lively atmosphere. He loved walking down its iconic boardwalk, a bustling stretch that attracted locals and tourists alike. He enjoyed watching the street performers, artists, and vendors. On his last visit there, as the day came to an end, he watched the stunning sunset over the Pacific Ocean. However, there were too many tourists. Then there was Beverly Hills. He wondered if any normal people lived there, as it was characterized by large, elegant homes, many of which are estates owned by celebrities and business magnates. There were so many interesting and unique areas, he knew he would enjoy the research. He also thought about where Sarah lived: Long Beach, which was more residential than other areas.

September arrived quickly. Sarah and Olivia were rushing around, Olivia trying to get dressed, not able to make up her mind what to wear, while Sarah made breakfast and packed a lunch. This was Olivia's first day of school. Sarah knew this was a big step for her, so she felt just as nervous.

"Hurry," said Sarah. "We don't want to be late." Never late for anything, the very thought of not getting somewhere on time made her perspire. Her mother always said, "If you are not five minutes early, you are late." She threw the last piece of toast in her mouth, grabbed her purse and car keys, and drove Olivia to the school. Olivia gave Sarah a kiss then climbed out of the car. Sarah waved, a warm feeling in her heart. *Is this how a mother feels?* She looked around. Yes, the mothers of the first-timers were waving and crying. *This is quite ridiculous, It's only school.* She brushed the tear from her face with the back of her hand and returned to the office.

Anne laughed as Sarah recounted the episode. All through the day, Sarah found it hard to concentrate and kept looking at the clock. At three, she was out the door, drove a little too fast, and took her place in the line of cars picking up kids. She was a little early but wanted to be in the front of the queue. It was a slow process. Sarah thought back to her school days; they took the bus no matter what kind of weather, and sometimes they even walked to school, but back then, it was a safer time in the world. Sarah saw Olivia and waved frantically. Olivia jumped in the car.

"So, how was your first day at school? Was it hard? Did you make any friends?

"Woah," said Olivia. "So many questions."

"I know," said Sarah, "I'm just excited."

"Well, I sat with three other girls, Mary, Sheila, and Laura, and we are besties. The teachers called us the four muska-something."

"They probably meant the four Musketeers."

"Who are they?"

Sarah said she would buy the book so she could read all about them and smiled when Olivia said the girls told her it was a movie.

"I met a boy."

"Oh, really? What's his name?"

"Roger. I actually met him at the mall when we went shopping."

Sarah remembered seeing her talking to a boy behind the stage. He looked a bit ragged.

"Is he in your class?"

"No, I think he goes to another school."

I have a feeling he doesn't go to any school, thought Sarah.

"What did he want?"

"Nothing. We were just shooting the breeze."

After the first week of school, it became a routine. Olivia enjoyed school immensely and joined lots of activities, like the gym club, and tried out for the soccer team. On the Monday of the third week, she asked if she could bring one of her friends home. Sarah stood against her car when Olivia arrived with a girl and a woman, presumably the mother. Olivia introduced them. "This is Sheila Cooke, and this is Mrs. Cooke, her mother." The ladies traded phone numbers and chatted briefly as Sheila and Olivia climbed into Sarah's car.

Sheila and Olivia didn't say anything on the drive home but kept bursting into fits of laughter. Sarah glanced in the rear-view mirror and couldn't help but wonder what was causing their amusement. Before they scurried up to Olivia's room, Sarah said, "Your friend doesn't say much."

Olivia looked at her and did some movements with her fingers.

"What are you doing?" asked Sarah.

"Duh. I just said, 'Hello, how are you?' in sign language."

"You know how to sign?"

"Well, Sheila is deaf, you know."

"No," said Sarah. "How come her mother didn't say anything to me?"

"Sheila doesn't want her to. That way, people don't feel sorry for her or treat her differently. She's been teaching me sign, and I love it. It's so easy."

"My God, Olivia, you never fail to amaze me. Let me go

make some dinner while you girls get serious and do your homework."

After a month of school, Sarah turned into a 'soccer mum,' driving six girls to practice and picking up Olivia from her various after-school activities. Sarah felt it would be nice to share this with Olivia's mother so called the mission.

"Hi, may I speak to Mary Wilson?"

"Mary who?" asked the administrator. "We have no one here with that name."

Sarah thought, *That lying scumbag, I have a good mind to go to that park and...*

Olivia interrupted her thoughts. "Sarah, where's my red T-shirt?"

"Well, I'm sorry, I haven't done the laundry yet. Time you learned to do your own. I'm not the maid, you know."

Olivia looked startled. Sarah did not often use that tone of voice. "Have I done something wrong?"

"Oh, I'm so sorry. Just a problem at work making me irritable." Sarah smiled and kissed Olivia on her head. *Now what? Will I have to go looking for Mary at the park again? Do I need to alert the judge or CPS?* Sarah slammed her hand down on the kitchen counter. *Everything was going well for Olivia and me. What if Mary tried to get her back? Surely, the judge wouldn't allow it.*

Olivia loved school and, despite lagging behind academically compared to her classmates, she dedicated herself to maintaining above-average grades by doing twice as much homework as needed. Sarah was proud of her and always encouraged her to take a break, especially when her favorite TV show was on. It was called *Enchanted Grove Gang,* and Olivia was fascinated.

"Maybe I will be an actor," she said one day.

"Believe me," said Sarah, "it's not as glamorous as you may think."

At school, Olivia was popular, not only with the girls but also among the boys, prompting a flicker of concern in Sarah. Was it time for 'the talk?' Reflecting on her own mother's avoidance on such matters of boys and sex, Sarah considered the importance of open communication and Sarah wondered how to approach such conversations with Olivia.

On Saturday mornings, Olivia would go to the office with Sarah, and Anne would teach her how to use the computer programs. Olivia loved to answer the phone, often in her best English accent, which always made Sarah laugh. Their weekends, filled with trips to the park, the mall, movies, and visits with friends, formed a close bond between Olivia and Sarah. Their friendly Scrabble and Boggle competitions, with Olivia's impressive vocabulary for her age, showcased her commitment to learning and growing.

One Sunday morning in early December, Olivia was working in her room on a school project. Sarah was having a late breakfast. She opened the fridge to get milk for her cereal. "Damn," she muttered. "It's sour. Olivia, come on. We have to go to the store for some milk."

"Aw, do I have to go?"

"Yes. I'm not leaving you alone."

"Why?"

"You're too young to be on your own."

"Duh! I was on my own tons of times before I lived with you."

Sarah looked at Olivia. She was right, but she still felt uncomfortable leaving her alone. *Why? What could happen to her? She's a good kid.* Besides the incident at the mall, she hadn't gotten into trouble. Kids her age are left alone in the house all the time. When Sarah was ten years old, she had a key to the door as her mother didn't get home until after school was out. Sarah hesitated. "Okay. You win. I'll be back in fifteen minutes."

The only store open that early was just a little bit too far away to walk. She picked up her keys and hurried to her car. The convenience store was unusually busy for a Sunday morning. Sarah waited in line impatiently with her milk and Olivia's favorite Dove chocolate bar. The clerk, seemingly in no hurry, was telling the customer in front of Sarah a joke. He laughed out loud and turned to look at her.

"I didn't get it," said Sarah. "I'm sorry, but I'm in a hurry. Could you ring these up for me?" She handed him the milk and chocolate bar.

Sarah climbed back into her SUV knowing she should be more patient, but she dealt with difficult people every day in her agency, so on Sundays she liked a day off.

She arrived back home, and as she turned the key in the door, she yelled, "Olivia, I have your favorite chocolate. Come and get it."

No answer. Okay, Sarah thought, she's playing her favorite game with me. Olivia would hide and then pounce out of a newly found hiding spot to surprise Sarah, or she pretended to have laryngitis and didn't speak for fifteen minutes but always broke down when Sarah cracked a joke.

"Well, I guess I'll just have to eat your chocolate instead of my cereal." Still no answer.

"Okay, tell me, how do elephants climb down trees? Mmm, you don't know. Well, they sit on a leaf and wait for autumn." No laughter. Now, Sarah was really worried. That joke, stupid as it may be, always made her laugh.

"Olivia, I'm coming into your room." Sarah opened the door slowly, as Olivia liked to hide behind the door. "Gotcha!"

She wasn't there. "Olivia, this is not funny. Where the hell are you?"

Sarah's heart beat faster. She looked under the bed, in the closet, and in the bathroom. No Olivia. Sarah moved into her own bedroom, where she saw the note.

Hi Sarah, I just thought about my mother and decided to take her some food, as I know where she will be right now. I'll be back soon. Olivia

Oh, my God, why on earth would she do that. As far as Olivia knew, her mother was in rehab. Sarah grabbed her bag to go look for her, but as she was leaving, she saw Olivia walking down the street. She was relieved to see her, but Olivia had to learn not to leave the house like that. "Olivia, where the hell have you been?"

"To the park. You know. I left you a note."

"Why? Your mother..."

"Yeah, I know; she's supposed to be in rehab."

"How do you know she isn't?"

"I heard you tell Anne."

"I guess I will have to be careful what I say in the future."

Olivia gave Sarah a tight hug, whispering, "I'm sorry."

"Well, young lady, if you ever do that again, I'll ground you for six months. If you need to go there, I will take you. It is not a safe place to be."

"Okay, I said sorry. I wasn't thinking. I promise I'll always tell you where I'm going."

They sat, had breakfast, did a little housework, and then sat down to watch the movie *Frozen* for the umpteenth time. Sarah didn't mind, as she enjoyed the songs, especially when Olivia sang along with them. Sarah had arranged for voice lessons the following week.

The days passed peacefully. Sarah's business was doing well. Olivia was enjoying her new life, and Sarah enjoyed being a mum.

24

At three-fifteen, as usual, Sarah jumped up, closed her laptop, said goodbye to Anne, and climbed in her car to get to Olivia's school. Ten minutes before arriving, the traffic came to a halt. Sarah looked around then tapped the button on her GPS for an alternative route. There was none. Annoyed at being late, she turned the radio to the traffic station. Due to an accident, she was trapped and could do nothing but wait.

Sarah drummed her fingers on the steering wheel and looked around to see a way out. Traffic was slow on the other side of the median because of the lookey-loos, but at least it was moving. Sarah honked her horn but was rewarded by several rude gestures from other drivers. She called Olivia on her Smartwatch. It just rang and rang. Then she called the school administrator, who informed her that she had already told the children to be patient if waiting for a ride. The traffic finally cleared, and Sarah sped to the school. She couldn't see Olivia, so she climbed out of her car and walked to the school entrance. There was still no sign of Olivia. She asked the school administrator, who told her Olivia had been chatting with her friends outside by the gate. The administrator thought maybe one of the other mothers had taken her home.

"Damn," said Sarah, "I wonder why she is not answering her

smartphone."

She urgently reached out to all of Olivia's friends' parents, but none had any information about her whereabouts. *Why isn't she answering her phone?* Returning home, there was still no sign of Olivia. Now, panic set in. She could feel her heart pounding, each beat echoing the growing fear.

The only choice she had was to report it to the police. She wrote a quick note in case Olivia returned in her absence and drove hurriedly to the nearest police station. Once there, Sarah provided a detailed report to an officer. Typically, missing persons reports had to wait for forty-eight hours, but an exception was made for children. The officer, showing empathy as a parent himself, assured Sarah that he would assign two of his best detectives to the case right away.

"Sit down, you brat," yelled the driver.

Olivia screamed back, "You almost jammed my finger in the window!"

"I will jam both hands if you don't shut up," replied the stranger.

Olivia slumped back into the seat of the SUV, forcing back the tears. She didn't want to look weak and wondered what had just happened. Her teacher had told the girls that their rides would be late due to an accident and just to wait inside the gates. Olivia had been chatting to her friends when she saw her mother lurking a little way down the street.

"I'll be right back," Olivia told her friends and walked towards her mother, who was talking to a man that Olivia did not recognize. She watched some kind of exchange go on between the two of them. She looked at her mom and knew right away that she was high on something. "Hi, Mom, what's up?"

"Nothing, kid, just came to see ya."

"Oh, I...." Before Olivia could complete her sentence, the man seized her, forcefully throwing her into the back of the SUV. With a swift motion, he tore off her Smartwatch, crushing it beneath the weight of his heavy boot. He jumped into the driver's seat, and Olivia lurched forward as the vehicle accelerated, the screech of tires marking a sudden and not-so-quiet departure.

She sat trembling, not from the cold but from fear, and held on tight to a rail to avoid being thrown around anymore. She looked out of the tinted windows and tried to figure out where they were going. Nothing looked familiar. She couldn't stop the tears as they rolled uncontrollably down her cheeks. About thirty minutes later, the car came to a screeching halt, and the door was flung open. A hood was put over her head, and she was led into a cold, echoing chamber. The darkness beneath the hood added to her disorientation, and she fought the urge to vomit. Her breath slowed, and her stomach had butterflies. She felt more scared than she had ever felt in her short life.

Sarah sat in her car, tears streaming down her face as guilt tugged relentlessly at her insides. If only this, if only that, she thought, overwhelmed by the situation. "What should I do?" she whispered to herself. After a few minutes, she turned on the ignition and drove to the park. Sarah settled on the same bench where she had first met Olivia, her mind drifting back to that day. Olivia was such a sweet child, and the mere thought of anything happening to her sent shivers down her spine.

Suddenly, the sharp sound of someone yelling pierced the air, jolting Sarah from her thoughts. She looked up to see a man and a woman engaged in a heated argument. Her heart raced with realization. "Oh, my God," she thought, "That's Olivia's mother." Without hesitation, Sarah sprang to her feet and ran toward them.

"Mary, have you seen Olivia?"

"Who?"

"Your bloody daughter," said Sarah, observing Mary's bloodshot eyes. "What are you on?"

"Huh!"

"You are absolutely stoned, you moron." Sarah grabbed Mary's shoulders in a fury and shook her hard. Something dropped to the ground. Sarah looked down and saw a plastic bag and a huge roll of twenty-dollar bills. "Where did this come from?" she asked as she picked up the money.

"None of your damn business."

"If this has anything to do with Olivia...."

"She sold the damn kid," said the guy she was arguing with.

"What?"

"Yeah, even I wouldn't do that. No matter how much I needed a fix."

"Mary, look at me. Who did you sell her to?" Sarah insisted.

"He didn't exactly give me his name and address," Mary said, laughing.

"This is serious, Mary. Think. Think hard."

"Oh, he drove a big black car. He looked Hispanic. That's all I remember. So, give me my stuff back."

Sarah was tempted to keep it but decided Mary could overdose as far as she was concerned. She obviously did not go to rehab. She immediately called the police and provided them with the information. Mary and the guy took off.

"Come back here," yelled Sarah. Despite being under the

24

influence of drugs, they sprinted away with surprising agility. Now, Sarah was really mad and thought, that woman will never get her daughter back if I have anything to do with it.

Back home, Sarah tried to relax with an herbal tea. It almost fell out of her hand when she heard a knock at the door. She peeked through the peephole.

"Who is it?"

"Detective Donaldson and Detective Mannet."

"Show me your ID, please." Two golden ovals with police insignia flashed across her field of vision. Sarah unlatched and opened the door.

Detective Donaldson was clean-cut, short hair, blue eyes, and in a decent suit. Detective Mannet, on the other hand, was unshaven with longer hair and crumpled clothes and reminded her of Colombo, the detective on a TV show.

"Ms. Sarah Houghton?"

"Yes, sir, that's me."

"We'd like to ask you a few questions about your missing child. We checked out the park, but the woman you described wasn't found."

"Right. She's obviously in hiding, as she knows I'm onto her. Also, Olivia's not my daughter. I'm her foster mom."

Nodding, Detective Mannet asked, "Do you have a recent picture?"

Sarah pulled out a picture from her desk. She looked at it lovingly, wiping back the tears. It had been taken on the first day Olivia had started school. She handed it to Detective Mannet.

"Are you sure her mother was telling the truth, or was she just being dramatic? Maybe the kid decided to go back on the streets."

"Didn't you read the report?" Sarah asked, her voice tinged with frustration. She took a deep breath to compose herself. "Olivia was genuinely happy here. Living with her drug-addicted mother was incredibly tough on her, especially when she was left to fend for herself most of the time. She used to tell me how lucky she felt to be here with me."

"Yeah," continued the detective a little unsympathetically, "But you know these streetwise kids often stray from what is considered good for them. They like the excitement of the streets. Maybe she took off, then some pervert picked her up."

Sarah held back her temper. "Olivia was not like that. She was different from most kids. Also, one of the guys in the park told me her mother had sold Olivia."

"Well, he's probably just a drunk. Maybe he was making it up," said the other detective.

Sarah stood up and studied the detectives. *Do these guys really care? Or are they just robotically doing their damn job?* She held back her temper, took a deep breath, and calmly said, "Really? In that case, what was her mother doing with all that cash?"

"Interesting. Well, as soon as we find her, we'll bring her in for questioning. We'll let her sober up and get the truth from her. Also, copies of Olivia's photo will be distributed to all the squad cars."

Detective Mannet handed her his card. "If you think of anything else, call me day or night."

Sarah closed the door. She knew in her heart that Olivia wouldn't willingly go anywhere with a stranger. She slumped down on the sofa, her mind racing. What kind of person would pay money for a child? This is America! Such horrors were supposed to be confined to third-world countries. But then again, desperation drove people to unimaginable lengths.

Addicts would do anything for their next fix, and trafficking children was a lucrative business. Sadly, this atrocity was happening everywhere, even in places you would least expect.

Sarah realized that dwelling on these thoughts would get her nowhere. She hastily grabbed a sweater and her keys. The urge to go out and search was strong, but she glanced at her phone, which needed charging. Fearful of missing a call from the police, she reluctantly nixed the idea. She paced up and down in her living room and decided it would be best to try and relax. She opened up her laptop but found it hard to concentrate on anything. *What if the police were right, and she had left willingly? No, impossible, she loved living here.*

Her mobile phone rang. Sarah grabbed it and hit 'accept call.' It was Detective Mannet.

"Miss Houghton, I'm just calling to let you know that the case has been taken over by the FBI. They should be sending someone over shortly, so please stay home."

Sarah sighed with relief, realizing that it would now be a greater priority under their control.

Local law enforcement agencies, such as the LAPD, typically assume the primary responsibility for investigating and overseeing missing child cases within their jurisdiction. But they collaborate with other agencies, including the FBI, when necessary. Detective Mannet felt this was one of those times and had exercised his discretion to notify the them, guided by his belief in a potential connection to one of their ongoing cases.

In a dimly lit, high-security conference room at the FBI headquarters in Washington, D.C., FBI Director Mitchell Barnes sat across from his top agent, Special Agent Roy Johnson. The tension in the room was palpable as they delved into the details of a pressing case involving another missing child and the possibility of human trafficking increasing in California.

Director Barnes, a seasoned figure with a stern demeanor, leaned forward, his fingers steepled in front of him. "Johnson, bring me up to speed on the missing child case. What do we have?"

Agent Johnson, known for his unwavering dedication and sharp investigative skills, began outlining the facts. "Sir, it's an eleven-year-old girl named Olivia Wilson. She disappeared without a trace from her school in Los Angeles. We are looking for her biological mother for more information. We've collaborated closely with the LAPD on the other missing children cases, but unfortunately, the leads are thin.

The director nodded, his gaze fixed on the photo of Olivia. "So, you believe it to be a human trafficking ring?"

Johnson sighed, "Yes, sir. We've been monitoring some suspicious activities in the area that align with known trafficking patterns. The circumstances are pointing in that direction."

Barnes' expression hardened. "I need you to fly to Los Angeles immediately and head up the investigation. Mobilize our resources, coordinate with local law enforcement, and keep me informed at every step. We need to find this child, Olivia, and any of the others before it's too late."

Agent Johnson nodded in acknowledgment. "I've already authorized a task force for a joint operation." He turned to leave and hesitated. "Sir, there is an English guy who's consulting for us in Los Angeles. He apparently knows the mother, I mean foster mother, of the child. I wonder if we could include him on our task force?"

The director's eyes narrowed as he emphasized, "Sure, it deviates from the usual protocol, but we can consider making an exception provided that he adheres strictly to his designated boundaries."

The FBI maintains a fleet of aircraft, often unmarked or discreet, for law enforcement and national security activities. Agent Johnson was aboard one of them, absorbed in the file of the traffickers. On arrival in Los Angeles, he was swiftly taken to the local FBI office. After a brief meeting with all the staff, he introduced himself to Charles.

"I hear you know the foster mother."

"Yes," replied Charles, "I actually met her when I was investigating a case in Mexico."

"Alright, we've got the green light from the director to involve you in this investigation." Charles was gratified to learn of his inclusion.

"Okay," said Agent Johnson to his colleagues, "This limey and me are going to interview the foster mother."

A knock on the door interrupted Sarah's thoughts. "Who is it?"

"Charles," came the reply.

For the second time that night, she looked through the peephole and gasped as she found herself staring straight into Charles' blue eyes. For a moment, she forgot where she was as her knees weakened and her gut wrenched. She opened the door, and there was Charles, holding up an FBI ID. A tall, brawny man stood next to him, a gun holstered at his side and his badge hanging from a lanyard around his neck. "Agent Roy Johnson. And of course you know Agent Charles Benson. May we come in?"

Sarah held the door open. "Agent Benson?" she stammered, staring at Charles. "Oh, my God. What the hell are you doing here? How do you know anything about this? What are you even doing in the States?"

Charles smiled, "May we come in? I can explain everything."

Sarah invited them in, closed the door, and turned to look at them.

Agent Johnson coughed, a little bewildered by all her questions. "Why don't you sit down?" he said.

Sarah sat on the chair, and the agents sat next to each other on the sofa. Charles briefly explained his situation, and Sarah managed to calm herself.

"How rude of me. Can I get you something to drink?" she asked.

"A good strong cup of real English tea would go down well," said Charles. "I haven't had a decent cuppa in weeks."

"And you, Agent Johnson?"

"Coffee, if you have it, black."

Sarah ducked into the kitchen. She returned a few minutes later, placed the cups on the coffee table, and sat opposite the agents. She had to concentrate hard to hear what was being said as the thoughts entered her mind. *Am I dreaming? What is Charles doing here?*

Agent Johnson leaned in, speaking with a gentle tone, "I know you've shared everything with the LAPD, and we understand this is an incredibly difficult time for you. We're here to help in any way we can. Can you walk us through the events leading up to your child's disappearance?"

Sarah recounted everything that had happened since she first met Olivia as they listened intently, nodding here and there, taking notes. Agent Johnson did most of the talking. "Rest assured, the FBI is working closely with local law enforcement, and we have resources dedicated to this case. Your cooperation is invaluable. We will keep you updated on any developments.

Please don't hesitate to contact us if you remember anything else, or if there's anything you need. Our priority is to bring your child home safely."

"Thank you."

Charles then added, "We'll also contact the NCMEC.

"What's that?" said Sarah.

"The National Center for Missing & Exploited Children."

"Thanks," she said, looking at Charles. "I would appreciate all the help I can get."

Sarah, although upset, was very conscious of the effect he was having on her.

Agent Johnson moved to the door, "Maybe you need a few moments of privacy. I'll wait in the car."

"So, did you move here with your wife?" asked Sarah.

"No, she's still in London with the children."

"When we were in Mexico, you never even mentioned your wife," interrupted Sarah.

"I was undercover. I couldn't really talk about my personal life, but my wife and I were not officially together."

"So, I was just a pawn, or arm candy for your little masquerade?"

"No, I really had feelings for you, but after you left, I figured you weren't interested." Charles protested.

"If you say so," said Sarah. "But I really don't feel like discussing this right now."

Charles took her hand, "When we find Olivia, we'll go for dinner and talk things over. I'll be in touch on a regular basis, but let me know if you hear anything new."

"Okay," said Sarah, as she gently kissed Charles on the cheek. "By the way, did you ever find out what happened to Harry Whelan?"

"No, that bastard is still on the loose somewhere in Mexico. But I'm not giving up. I owe that much to Ricardo."

"Is he okay?"

"Yes," replied Charles, "He was shot, but he's fully recovered and enjoying his retirement."

Charles said goodbye, and Sarah walked back into the living room and flopped on the sofa. Seeing Charles again compounded the stress she was feeling. Memories of Mexico swam around her head as the image of Harry Whelan came into her vision, and she hoped that he was not in the US. Her thoughts were disturbed by the shrill of the telephone.

It was from a TV reporter named John Cameron, one of the top investigative reporters for ABC. Sarah was a fan of his work, and when he asked her to come to the studio, she counted herself lucky that he would be involved. He had heard the news over the police radio.

"So that's how you are always ahead with the news."

"No comment," said John. "Can you come to the studio tomorrow at ten a.m.?"

"Sure," said Sarah.

After a restless night, she arrived at the studio, where John's assistant greeted her. Apparently, he was out covering another story.

A makeup artist dabbed a little powder on Sarah's face while a sound technician hooked her up to a microphone. The producer decided to tape the interview instead of going live, as they only had four minutes in the segment. Sarah was relieved. She didn't feel comfortable enough to go the whole time without breaking down. It was important to make an impact in the four minutes allowed. Sarah hoped wherever Olivia was, she would see the show and possibly find her way home.

24

Those four minutes felt like ten, but when they were finished, the segment producer said, "That was good. Let's hope it can bring Olivia back."

Later, Sarah wandered aimlessly around the condo. She wasn't responsible for the situation, but if anything happened to Olivia, she would blame herself. *If only that traffic accident hadn't stopped me on the way to school,* she thought.

As the news flashed across her TV screen, Sarah was surprised that Cameron was heading the segment. It went on to say that four other girls ranging from nine to fourteen had disappeared in the past few months. Sarah felt a cold shiver go down her spine. *What's going on? Is there some serial pervert or murderer on the prowl, or is it human trafficking?* She felt sick.

25

Charles and Agent Johnson drove back downtown, each in their own thoughts. Charles couldn't get Sarah out of his mind. Seeing her again just confirmed he still had strong feelings for her. In Mexico, he knew she had feelings for him, but now it was obvious that she thought she had just been used. He hadn't meant to get involved with Sarah, but from the moment he had set eyes on her, he knew she was special. *I can't lose her for the second time.* If he and Sarah did have a relationship, he welcomed the idea of having Olivia as part of his family. He hadn't even met the girl, but from what Sarah described, she sounded like a delight. But first, he had to win Sarah over. His own children were old enough to accept any changes, and if things did work out, Olivia would have instant siblings. The thought of Olivia or any other child being in danger was devastating. He imagined one of his own children being in that position. It made him even more determined to find out who was running this trafficking ring and put an end to it.

Charles entered the precinct and sat at his desk, which was not tidy, but it was organized. As an intelligence analyst, he played a crucial role in gathering, analyzing, and interpreting information to support investigations and decision-making. Juggling three cases, he received a directive from Agent Johnson to prioritize the trafficking case. One of his roles was collaboration with law enforcement agencies and government entities; however, he couldn't shake the feeling that the CIA was not sharing all the necessary information.

Agent Sean McCallum, a short, burly man with a thick Irish accent, swept by Charles' desk, causing a windstorm big enough to blow the papers onto the floor. Apparently, he was a transplant from New York City five years ago and now, due to the shortage of agents, Charles had been assigned as his partner.

"I hear you have a special interest in that Long Beach case of the missing kid?"

"Yeah, I do. I knew Ms. Houghton a brief time when I was undercover in Mexico.

"Heard you lost your guy down there," he said.

Charles bit his lip to keep from saying something he might regret. He had only been with this unit a short while and had a lot to prove, especially being an Englishman from MI6. However, Agent Johnson had taken a liking to him and turned to the agent. "Give him a break, will ya. You don't know the whole story."

Charles sat and shuffled mindlessly through papers on his desk. His mind wandered back to the memories from Mexico. Harry Whelan. *That bastard. I was an idiot to think he was a friend. Instead, he is a drug dealer, kidnapper, and probably a murderer. I have a gut feeling he is also involved with child trafficking. I'll hunt him down 'til the day I die.*

At least, with the help he received from Ricardo, the authorities closed the smuggling ring and the Tequila Import Company. The leader, Manuel, would be in jail for many years. Harry remained as a lost thread. Sitting alone with his thoughts, Charles shook his head in frustration. He had a sneaky suspicion that Harry had moved to the US, but all manifests of flights from the UK to the US and from Mexico to the US had been checked, and Harry was not listed. Of course, he could have traveled under a pseudonym or driven across the US border with a false passport.

"Penny for your thoughts." Agent Johnson's six-foot frame hovered over Charles' desk. "It might help if you answered a phone now and then," he added, laughing.

"Sorry, mate, I was thinking about little Olivia and the danger she may be in."

Someone passed by his desk with a brown bag. It reeked of garlic, which made Charles realize how hungry he was. "I'm hungry, and the noise in this place makes it hard to concentrate," said Charles.

"Come on, let's get out of here. I know a great deli just down the road," said Agent Johnson. Charles didn't have to be told twice. He grabbed a file and followed the agent out.

Sarah showered. The water was a little hotter than usual, but she didn't notice. She felt numb. She haphazardly threw on some clothes, not caring how she looked, which was alien to her normal fastidious dress code. She pulled back her hair and left home without a trace of makeup. She arrived at the office, and her assistant Anne looked at her. "God, you look awful. Are you okay?"

"Olivia disappeared from school yesterday. I went to the park, and I think her mother handed her over to some child trafficking gang."

"Oh, no! What can I do to help?"

"Nothing right now, I guess. The police and FBI are looking

into it, and the local TV station will be doing another piece on the news tonight. I just came in to check my messages and answer a few emails. I want to be back at the condo later so they can set up my phone with a listening device in case I get a ransom call."

"This is all so surreal," said Anne, trying to keep the tears back. "Olivia's such a great kid. But that mother of hers is a real bastard. She took your money and ran. You know, Sarah, you must be less naive about this kind of thing."

"I'm learning."

Anne smiled weakly.

The only sound in the office was the clicking of keyboards. Thirty minutes later, Sarah sighed. "Well, I've done as much as I can. Would you mind looking after the office again?"

"No, not at all. You have enough on your plate right now. Go!"

"Thanks, you're such a good friend. I'll call you later, okay?"

Sarah returned to the park to see if she could get any more information. As she passed a clump of trees, she heard a voice. "Hey, miss."

She turned to see a young boy not much older than Olivia, maybe twelve or thirteen. He wore dirty, worn-out clothes, and his hair was matted. He looked familiar, but she couldn't think of where she might have seen him. "What do you want?" asked Sarah.

"I know something you might wanna hear," he replied.

"Oh yeah, like what?"

"How much ya gonna give me?"

"Well, let me see. How do you know who I am and what kind of information I need?"

"Me and my boys make it our business to know what's going

on around here."

Sarah forced a smile. "Your boys?"

"Yeah, me and my boys."

Sarah thought for a moment. "Why don't you tell me more about you and your boys."

"Like, er... we're all in a gang. Well, not really a gang, more like an organization."

"Like, the Mafia?" said Sarah.

"Nah, don't be such a retard."

Sarah thought this kid was way too mature for his age. He reminded her of the Artful Dodger from *Oliver Twist*.

The boy continued, "My boys are kids who run away from drunken dads and deadbeat mothers. They don't wanna go to group homes, so they find their way to my place. Got a really cool pad downtown."

"How do you survive?" asked Sarah.

"C'mon, lady, I'm not gonna tell ya everything. Don't want cops knocking on my door if you know what I mean."

"Of course not. So, what kind of information do you have for me?"

"It's about your daughter, Olivia."

"She's not my..." Sarah stopped herself, looked in her purse, and found forty dollars.

"How about twenty dollars?"

"How about forty?" he responded.

"Do you have X-ray vision?"

"Huh?"

"Never mind. Okay, forty." She held it tightly in her hand so he couldn't grab it and run. "Information first. I don't trust you, and what's your name?"

"It ain't important," he replied.

After a tasty lunch, Charles felt better. He sat at his desk once again and studied the case file. Four additional reports from mothers detailed their children as missing.

Agent McCallum walked over. "Come on, Limey, let's show you how we do it this side of the pond... and don't forget your gun," he said on the way out.

That wasn't such a dumb remark, as Charles usually didn't pack a gun back home. While some MI6 agents may receive weapons training, their primary role is not that of a traditional law enforcement officer. Whether they carry a gun or not would depend on the specific mission or situation. MI6 agents are more likely to work in cooperation with other intelligence and law enforcement agencies when an operation requires the use of firearms or other weapons.

Charles opened his desk drawer and pulled out the Glock 19 chambered in 9mm. The only time it had been fired in the last month was at the shooting range. He was an excellent shot but didn't care to demonstrate that talent in front of his new colleagues. He had also been trained as a sharpshooter. He followed Sean to an unmarked car. He hardly had time to put on the seat belt as Sean gunned the accelerator, doing 0-60 in about four seconds, lights flashing and dodging traffic, accompanied by another two agents in the car behind. Agent McAllum briefed him. They had received a tip about a drug drop. They arrived at the destination in fifteen minutes, which would normally take at least forty.

Charles got out the car. The blood had drained from his face; he was dizzy and felt sick. He inhaled deeply, then caught up with Sean.

"You don't look so good," said Sean with a slight smirk on his face.

"Very funny. You always drive like that?"

"You got a problem with that, Limey?"

"Listen, you Yank, I...."

Suddenly, shots were fired. They both ran into the apartment complex, guns drawn.

"You, come with me," Sean yelled to an Agent Lewis. "Charles, go with Agent Carter and cover the back entrance."

As Sean carefully advanced up the front steps, Charles made his way around to the back. The overgrown weeds threatened to trip him up, but he managed to avoid stumbling. Peering through a broken screen, he saw no one, but the sound of hushed voices made him cautious. Charles entered through the kitchen door, staying low, his gun at the ready. A hooded figure carrying a gun came into view, taking aim at Sean. In the nick of time, Charles fired a shot that struck the armed intruder in the leg. He ran towards him and swiftly disarmed the assailant and forced him to the ground.

Meanwhile, Sean kicked in the bedroom door but quickly lowered his gun as he was confronted by a woman who was sobbing and badly beaten, holding onto a crying child.

"He tried to steal my baby!" she yelled.

"Bastard. Maybe I should shoot him in the other leg," Charles growled.

Sean holstered his gun and began consoling the distressed woman while Charles secured the perpetrator in handcuffs. The injured man whimpered in pain. "Shut up," Charles warned, "or I'll hurt you even more."

An ambulance arrived to transport the assailant to the hospital, and another team showed up to take the mother and child to a safe haven. Sean and his team conducted a meticulous search of the apartment, uncovering only a few bundles of cocaine.

Sean felt a sense of disappointment, as the tip had suggested a larger quantity. In the car on the way to the station, he said, "Thanks, Limey. Some good shooting in there."

Charles just smiled. Maybe he would get a little more respect from Sean McCallum in the future. "What is with these guys beating up women?" asked Charles.

"Drugs," Sean replied angrily.

At the end of the shift, Sean asked if Charles wanted to have a drink at the local hangout.

"Thanks, maybe another time. There is something I need to do."

Charles checked his emails but found nothing that would help with Sarah's case. Among them were a couple from his kids, who were thoroughly enjoying their life but did say they missed their dad. Charles missed them too but looked forward to when they would visit him in the summer holidays. He also read some research on other cases involving missing children, noting that the internet was luring more vulnerable kids away than ever before. Sarah had mentioned that Olivia had a watch that allowed her to call home but didn't grant access to the internet, which he thought was a good idea. *So who had taken her?* His phone rang, and it was Sylvia. He hadn't heard from her since Mexico.

"Well, hello there. Long time no hear," Charles greeted her.

He and Sylvia had worked together many years ago in Paris. There had definitely been no romantic connection between them, as she was in a serious relationship with another woman. They had remained steadfast friends, always supporting each other.

"I have some important information for you," she said.

"Oh, and what might that be?"

"Harry Whelan is in the US. In fact, he's in California. Unfortunately, we lost track of him, so just be careful. You never know what he's capable of. His sister lives in the US, and we're trying to track her down, as Harry may be paying her a visit quite soon."

"Cheers, Sylvia. You always come through for me. Take care."

Charles hung up the phone and leaned back in his seat. *Harry, you bastard. I'll get you yet. Lucky break for me, you showing up in California.*

26

Sarah stood firmly and held the money in her hands. The boy stood there and scratched his head, shivering a little from the chilly wind. California winter was on its way. She hoped that wherever Olivia was, she was not hungry or cold. Sarah pulled her coat tighter, hugging herself, still holding onto the forty dollars.

"A real little entrepreneur, aren't you?" said Sarah.

"Yup. Gotta make a living. I was down on San Pedro docks with some of me boys. We saw this guy going into one of the warehouses. Then a big crane moved a few of the containers."

"What's the containers got to do with anything?"

"Me and my boys seen 'em get moved but never get on ships like the other ones. Maybe they're hiding something inside or someone."

Sarah gasped, then thought, What if these kids are acting as lookouts for these criminals, and they're getting paid from both sides? She then pushed that thought to one side. *God! I've been watching too many movies.*

"You realize I'm going to have to call the FBI about all this?"

"Sure, but when they get here, we'll scarper."

"By the way, how do you know Olivia?" asked Sarah.

"Well, we..."

"Wait a minute. I remember. You were talking to her at the mall, and then I saw you at her school. She told me about you. Your name is Roger."

"Yep, that's me."

"Did you see her at the docks?"

"No, but I saw some other guys with some scruffy-looking kids. They looked like Mexicans except this one. I took a picture." He showed Sarah.

"Oh, my God." *It's Harry. His hair is less red, but that's definitely him.* "Email that to me, please."

"Duh! How about a text? You do know how to text?"

"I'm not that old," said Sarah as she handed the boy another twenty dollars with a stern warning, "Don't you dare tell anyone about this, or I'll make sure you and your boys end up in juvie."

The boy, with a cocky demeanor, replied, "You would never find us, lady! We're smarter than you think." With that, he disappeared as quickly as he had appeared.

Sarah forwarded the information and picture to Charles then called him. "His new look," she said.

Charles responded with urgency, "Don't go anywhere near the docks. Damn, so he did make it over the border. I wonder what name he's using. It looks like the bastard has got involved with child trafficking. But, Sarah, don't worry, we'll get right down there and have Olivia back before you know it."

Sarah sat at the coffee house, barely aware of her surroundings, and stared at the picture the boy had sent her. Somehow, she trusted him. She puckered her lips. Her face muscles tightened. Harry looked even uglier than she remembered, especially with his badly dyed hair. Gulping down the dregs of her latte, she paid and hurried out.

She knew Harry was capable of anything, so wouldn't put it past him to be running a child trafficking organization. Sarah even considered buying a gun but was afraid she might just shoot Harry on sight, especially if he had harmed Olivia in any way. She was tempted to drive to the docks, but Charles had been very specific about that. After the two lattes, she was so wired she took a walk down Belmont Shore. She jumped when her cell rang. It was just Anne checking up on her.

"Thanks for calling, Anne. Charles and his men are at the docks right now, checking out those containers. I can't concentrate, so you'll have to handle the office for the next few days.

"Okay, no problem," replied Anne.

The container enveloped Olivia in darkness and dampness, and the pungent odor reminded her of the inebriated men who used to hang around her mother. She stretched her legs as much as the confined space allowed, and her feet collided with the container's side. Boxes lined up in front restricted her from fully straightening her legs, and she nervously hoped they were secure, not wanting them to tumble onto her. Amidst a throbbing headache and foggy thoughts, Olivia asked herself: *Where am I?*

Someone coughed.

"Hello. Hello, who's there?" cried Olivia.

Out of the shadow, a young girl's face, barely visible, appeared on the far side of the container.

"Who are you?" asked Olivia.

A weak voice replied, "*Yo soy Yolanda. Tu hablas Espanol?*

Olivia thought a moment, then said, "Me, Olivia, *no habla Espanol.*" Olivia thought about those Spanish classes that she never enjoyed at school and ended up daydreaming instead of learning. "*No mucho. Donda esta...* here. Dang. This is hard," mumbled Olivia.

"It's okay, I speak little English."

"Better than my Spanish," said Olivia, feeling embarrassed.

"I come to America with mama's *amiga* to work for rich *familia,*" Yolanda said, sniffling back the tears. "I will work hard for money to send *mi casa,*" she continued.

"Well, please try to stay strong. I will help you."

"*Tambien*," whispered Yolanda.

Olivia had heard about this kind of thing from one of her teachers. These trafficking organizations brought children from Mexico or India and made them work for no money. But why me? I'm American, thought Olivia. She was getting hotter and hotter. Her hair stuck to the back of her neck. She found a tissue in her pocket, but it didn't help. Her mouth was dry. She tried to lick her lips to no avail. At that moment, the container shook and swung from side to side, tossing her and Yolanda around, moving some boxes dangerously close to them. It felt like they were being lifted into the air. They desperately hung on to each other. The noise of an engine squealing and the jangling of chains was so loud, and the stench of diesel fuel made Olivia feel sick. Just before the container landed, Olivia was thrown to one side and bumped her head. A little blood trickled down her face. Then, they were on the move. It was a bumpy ride. It felt like an eternity before they stopped. Outside was dark when the doors opened. A man entered and threw hoods over their heads, then shoved them into the back of a car.

After a long drive, Olivia heard a squeal that sounded like iron gates grinding open and crunching from some gravel. They were grabbed by their shoulders and roughly escorted into a building. The hoods were whipped off, catching some of Olivia's hair. "What is wrong with you people? You just hurt me!" she yelled, straightening her ponytail, her fear overcome by anger.

"What have we got here?" said a woman, grabbing Olivia by the shoulders. Maybe I should shave your head, and you won't have that problem. So shut your mouth and behave. And no more wise remarks. Understood?"

Olivia shook her head. They were standing in a huge kitchen, and her stomach growled. A short conversation in Spanish between the man and the woman was too quiet for either them to hear. Olivia didn't recognize the man. He wasn't from the park. He wore nice clean clothes and was tall, but his strong aftershave made Olivia gag. The woman had bags under her eyes, which made her look old and tired. She was dressed in a plain black dress, and her hands were rough and calloused. The man left, and the woman said, *"Venga,"*

Olivia and Yolanda followed her to a narrow room that housed two single beds and a dingy light. The woman said a few words to Olivia.

"I'm American. I don't speak Spanish."

"Well, you better learn fast," replied the woman, slapping Olivia on the head. "And I told you, no more wise remarks, or you'll regret it."

"Where's the bathroom?" asked Olivia. The woman laughed as she pointed to a pot under the bed.

"Pig," Olivia muttered.

"What did you say?'

"Not very big."

"I'll bring you some food in a few minutes," said the woman

and closed the door. Olivia heard the key turn. She shook the handle. They were prisoners. Yolanda began to cry. Olivia guessed she must be a year younger than her. She felt sorry for the girl so put her arm around her and stroked her hair. "Don't worry, I have people looking for me. We'll be rescued."

The woman returned with some flannel nightshirts and Menudo soup, which Olivia hated, but hunger got the best of her. "I've set the alarm for five a.m.," said the woman as she left. Once more, the door was bolted.

Olivia and Yolanda finished the soup. Olivia tucked Yolanda into bed, then looked through the tiny, barred window. The three-quarter moon ducked in and out of the clouds as she sobbed quietly.

It had rained the day before. Charles and Sean methodically traversed the dock area, their boots amassing mud with each careful step. Their eyes scanned the litter-strewn surroundings. Armed with a partial container number provided by the boy's information, they homed in on specific containers, yet their search yielded no traces of life amid the ones investigated. Charles picked up a tattered teddy bear. He grimaced as he thought about how he would feel if this happened to his own children. Frustrated and angry, he kicked a container with his muddy boot. *What if this kid Roger is leading us on a wild goose chase?* He scoured the area once more when something caught his eye. He bent down and picked up a muddy object that had been wedged in the ground. He carefully scraped off the dirt and recognized it as a Browning A-bolt, a component of a sophisticated rifle.

"I think this is a lot more than child trafficking," Charles remarked, holding up the A-bolt. "Look what I found."

26

Sean took the A-bolt and nodded grimly. "Damn, they're gun-running as well. I wouldn't put it past that creep Harry Whelan. Maybe the kids are just a cover-up for the gun smuggling."

"Could be," agreed Charles, "Kidnapping certainly would keep us distracted from their real business. Very clever. Bastards!"

"I'll bring in the forensic team," Sean suggested. "They should be able to find more evidence of what's really going on here. Maybe you and I need to have a talk with the customs officials. Someone's turning a blind eye."

As they gathered more information and pieced together the puzzle, it became clear that the situation was far more complex and dangerous than they had initially imagined.

27

Sarah waited for Charles at the diner as she stared at the TV screen and watched the footage of an explosion. "Oh, God, I like that reporter. I hope he wasn't injured," she said to the waitress.

"Thanks. I appreciate the compliment coming from such a beautiful woman," said a man coming towards her.

Sarah blushed as she turned to see the reporter from the footage. Dark curls hung over his broad forehead. His brown eyes embraced her.

What a strange coincidence he is in the same coffee shop as I am. "I thought you were hurt in the explosion?" said Sarah.

"Thank you for being concerned." He extended his hand. "Johnny Walker, pleased to meet you."

"Johnny Walker; you are kidding, right?"

"No. Either my parents had a serious sense of humor or were drinking it at the time of my birth. My friends call me JW."

"But I thought your name was John Cameron?"

"That's my name on air. The studio didn't think the public would take me seriously with my real name," he said, laughing.

Even though his laugh was contagious, Sarah could only force a smile. "I apologize for being so forward, but remember that piece you did on child trafficking? It was my child that prompted it. I have a little more information now, and I wonder if you could help me."

He sat on the next chair to her. She leaned closer to him, catching the subtle scent of his aftershave. Blushing slightly, she backed off a little and gave him an embarrassed smile while showing him the text and video from Roger.

"Interesting," he said. "Is this source reliable?

"I think so," said Sarah hopefully. After all, his other information had been correct.

"I am on a deadline right now, so let's meet later, and you can tell me the whole story. Meanwhile, I'll have my investigator check it out. He's the best around, and if there is something to be found, he's the man to find it."

This provided a glimmer of hope for Sarah. JW handed her a business card and, understanding the urgency of her need for help, said he would make it his priority. As he swiftly departed, Sarah clutched the business card tightly, feeling a mix of gratitude and relief. Under alternate circumstances, she entertained the idea that she might have engaged in a bit of playful flirtation with the handsome and robust man.

"Who was that?" asked Charles as he approached her table.

"Oh, just a reporter," said Sarah, still smiling.

"He looked very friendly. How long have you known him?" asked Charles.

Sarah resented this line of questioning. "What has that got to do with anything?"

"You never know," said Charles. "Sometimes children are abducted by people they know very well."

"Well, rest assured, she has never met Mr. Walker. He's an investigative reporter, and he is showing special interest in Olivia's case."

"Oh, really? Personally, I thought he was showing special interest in you."

"Charles, stop acting like a jealous lover."

"Not jealous, just concerned."

"Right," said Sarah. "So, tell me, any more news from the docks?"

"No, nothing yet, but we are doing a thorough investigation, trying not to piss off the Port Authorities." He stood silent for a moment, then said, "Why don't you have dinner with me tonight so we can discuss some of the details of this case?"

"I'm sorry, I can't make tonight."

It would have been nice to relax and catch up, but Sarah was just not ready. With a parting kiss on the cheek, Charles bid her farewell, and Sarah was left alone once again, her thoughts consumed by worry and the relentless quest to find Olivia. She opened her laptop and read through some emails. What was she hoping for? A message from Olivia saying she would be back soon. One from Roger saying he had found Olivia's whereabouts. She wished it was all just a bad dream and she would wake up at any moment.

As Sarah contemplated the sudden void left by Olivia's disappearance, she reflected on her own life. At thirty-two, she had no children, no boyfriend, and no husband. Olivia had been more than just a girl she cared for; she had been a source of inspiration and, in many ways, the closest thing to a child Sarah had ever known. She was so glad she had made the decision to become a foster mom and the subsequent outcome. Without it, she pondered where Olivia might be now—perhaps in a safer environment or on drugs like her mother. Then, an unsettling thought crossed her mind about Harry. Could his actions be driven by revenge for what happened in Mexico, or was it just a coincidence?

She felt a burning sensation in her stomach and a throbbing migraine. Olivia had really matured during her time under Sarah's care. The girl possessed a strong will, a determination to turn her life around, and a glimmer of hope for the future.

Sarah knew that Olivia had been taken against her will. It was inconceivable that she would willingly leave; she loved living with Sarah. But the questions remained: Where was Olivia now? Was she safe? These thoughts haunted Sarah as she glanced at the clock, realizing that she needed to return home, freshen up, and gather her thoughts before meeting with JW. Hopefully, his investigator would be able to find vital information about Olivia and the other children's disappearances.

For the next couple of days, Olivia and Yolanda settled into a daily routine. Their mornings began early, at five a.m., with a measly breakfast of oatmeal. The bulk of their morning was dedicated to housecleaning, a task that kept them occupied until noon. After their diligent cleaning routine, they would take a break for lunch, often enjoying leftovers from the main kitchen. It was a simple meal, but Olivia appreciated every bite. The remainder of their day was spent on more housecleaning tasks. Olivia had never encountered such a large house before; it consisted of an astounding thirty-four rooms. The mansion was perched atop a hill, secluded and without any neighbors in sight. Olivia learned that this grand estate belonged to the wealthy George family. They had four children, who were expected to return from boarding school in the coming weeks. More work, thought Olivia. The sheer size and seclusion of the mansion left her with a sense of awe and curiosity. Little did she know that her life was about to take a dramatic and unsettling turn, leading her down a path filled with uncertainty and danger.

As Olivia continued her daily chores, the constant flow of visitors loading and unloading boxes into vans became a routine part of her life. Among the many faces she encountered, one man stood out, and not for the right reasons. He frequently visited the mansion and would often fixate on Olivia, his unsettling stares sending waves of discomfort through her.

One fateful day, as Olivia was diligently dusting, a sudden chill ran down her spine, making her skin prickle with unease. She couldn't ignore the sensation, and she turned around to find that very man engaged in conversation with a woman she had never seen before. As she observed the scene, he cast a sly smile her way while gently caressing his girlfriend's hand. The sight was enough to send chills through Olivia's frail body. Her sharp instincts told her to distance herself from this unnerving encounter. She quietly slipped out of the room, hovering near the door, hidden from view but still curious about the nature of their visits. From her vantage point, she could still hear and see them. The man combed his hair and looked in the mirror. The woman came close to him. "You look so handsome."

Olivia screwed up her face, stifling a laugh. In her eyes, he was nowhere close to handsome.

The man spoke to the woman. "Thank you, sweetie. By the way, I must go visit my sister in that clinic. She's using again after her divorce. I won't be long. Why not meet me back at my apartment?"

Olivia discreetly watched them as they exchanged a few parting words. He picked up his keys, preparing to leave, and turned to her. "*Me voy*, Ana."

"Harry, darling, please, let us speak English," Ana

responded, in an insistent tone, "I'm in the US now and want to blend in. I need to practice."

Harry acquiesced, replying, "Okay, my sweet. See you later."

Ana leaned in and kissed him affectionately, and as he started to turn away, he playfully suggested, "Let's just speak Spanish in the bedroom. It turns me on."

These words, overheard by Olivia, added another layer of repulsiveness to her opinion involving this enigmatic couple. She couldn't help but wonder about the secrets they might be hiding. Olivia ran down to the kitchen, hoping she hadn't been noticed. She was starving so grabbed a roll on her way out.

A week later, Beatriz, who was also a young Mexican girl who helped Mrs. George assigned Olivia to tackle the weeding task in the large garden. Olivia stepped outside and breathed in the fresh air. The sunlight felt like a temporary respite from the mansion's confines. In a moment of hopeful optimism, Olivia considered that her captors might be beginning to trust her, which raised a glimmer of possibility for escape. But as she worked in the garden, she couldn't help but voice her concerns to Beatriz. "Why do you work for these horrid people?" Olivia whispered.

Beatriz's reaction was swift and stern. "How dare you be so insolent! If Mrs. George hears you ask questions like that, you'll be in trouble."

Olivia glanced back at the imposing mansion and then back to Beatriz. She pressed further, determined to understand the situation. "What kind of trouble would I be in?"

Beatriz hesitated, her gaze darting nervously around the garden. She then leaned closer to Olivia and whispered, "She may beat you."

The gravity of the situation became clear to Olivia. Beatriz,

201

like herself, was trapped in this nightmarish circumstance, with no apparent hope of escaping.

"They pay me a small wage so I can send money back to Mexico, and they know where my family live. If I don't do as they say, they tell me some harm may come to them."

Olivia's heart sank as she realized the extent of the control and manipulation her captors exercised over both her, Yolanda and Beatriz. Escape from this situation would prove to be far more challenging and perilous than she had initially imagined.

As Olivia continued to impress her captors with her gardening skills, they allowed her to tend to the garden once again the following day. The routine work provided her with an opportunity, albeit a risky one. A van parked nearby drew her discreet attention. Olivia watched individuals unload wooden boxes, and when Beatriz entered the mansion, the driver followed her inside. With sweat pouring down her sunburned face, Olivia cautiously moved closer to the van. After a quick scan of her surroundings, she jumped inside the vehicle and hastily pulled a tarp over herself, trying to blend in with the cargo as much as possible. A couple of tense minutes passed, and the driver closed the back door. She heard the driver's door slam shut. The engine roared to life, and the van began to move. Olivia had no idea where they were headed, but at that moment, the feeling of freedom outweighed any uncertainty. As the van navigated the streets, Olivia clung to a spare tire to prevent herself from crashing into the sides of the vehicle with every turn. Her heart raced with a mix of fear and the hope that she would soon be free.

Sarah entered the coffee bar and saw JW sitting at a corner table. As she approached, he stood up, smiled, and pulled out the chair for her. She was nervous and excited to chat with him because, throughout his career, he had broken numerous high-profile stories that had led to the dismantling of other child trafficking networks and the rescue of countless victims. His investigative prowess, unwavering determination, and dedication to fact-checking and accuracy had earned him the respect of both his peers and law enforcement agencies. "What would you like to drink?' he asked.

"Better make it a decaf latte. I'm already having problems sleeping."

JW went up to the counter and bought two coffees.

Sarah sat and sipped on the hot coffee while she retold the story of Olivia's disappearance. JW scribbled on his notepad. He asked a few more questions and scribbled again.

"Don't you use a recorder or an iPad?" asked Sarah.

"I prefer speed writing."

Sarah was dismayed with his approach and stole a quick glance at his odd squiggles and abbreviations. When they finished, JW looked over his notes, added some more, put down his pen, and looked solemnly at Sarah. "I don't want to alarm you, but this sounds like it might have something to do with an organization I've been investigating for months."

"What do you mean?" asked Sarah, grasping her paper coffee cup a little too tightly.

"I've been talking with a group called Polaris Project, a non-profit that runs the national human trafficking hotline.

"Human trafficking?" gasped Sarah.

"Yes," said JW. "Unfortunately, the US Department of State estimates this business to be a thirty-two-billion-dollar global industry with up to seventeen thousand victims yearly. It's horrible to consider that this is the world's third most profitable criminal enterprise behind drugs and arms."

"My God. What are you saying? Olivia might have been taken by these people?"

"Maybe, maybe not," replied JW.

"Isn't the government doing anything about it?"

"Actually, today, there are more people aware of it, so we have more police, more FBI, and more media working to shine a light on this tragedy and get it stopped."

"Apparently, not fast enough," said Sarah. The initial realization that Olivia might be in the hands of child traffickers left Sarah in a state of shock. She had heard plenty. Her face drained of color. She held her stomach, afraid she might throw up.

JW continued, "Polaris has reported a huge increase since 2010. So that is worrying me because the next step after maid service is using these children as sex slaves."

"Oh, my God," Sarah whispered, her voice trembling with shock and disbelief. The words were barely audible, but they carried the weight of a thousand emotions. In that moment the grim possibility of Olivia being taken by child traffickers hung heavily in the air, leaving her paralyzed with dread.

JW placed his hand on hers. "I'm sorry, Sarah, but I had to let you know the worst possible scenario."

"I know," said Sarah." Olivia is a strong-willed little girl but no match for these monsters. Is there anything I can do?"

"Well, there's a group of volunteers who print and distribute fliers. Maybe you could help them. They can also offer you moral support."

"I will. I'll do anything to help."

They sat in silence, finishing their coffee, until JW said, "I must go. I have a deadline. You have my card, so don't hesitate

27

to call if you need a shoulder to cry on, anytime, day or night."

"Thanks."

Sarah wandered home in a daze.

28

As the van continued its journey, Olivia sensed a gradual reduction in speed, offering her some relief from the turbulent ride. However, her newfound hope was abruptly shattered when the van screeched to a sudden halt. Panic surged as the back door swung open. The tarp that covered her was ripped off to be met with the chilling sight of a gun pointed directly at her, held by an enraged driver who wasted no time in demanding her presence.

"Get out," he yelled.

A blue sedan pulled up, and before she could react, she was violently grabbed by her tiny arms by one of the guards she had seen at the mansion. Pain shot through her as he roughly shoved her into the back of the car. The impact caused her to bang her head against a metal container sitting on the back seat, leaving her disoriented and dizzy. Through blurred vision, she looked at the man before she fell unconsciousness.

A harsh slap to the face jolted Olivia back to consciousness. Her vision cleared, revealing the menacing figure of Mrs. George, who stood before her with hands on her hips and an angry scowl on her face. Next to her, Beatriz appeared terrified and helpless. Mrs. George's anger knew no bounds as she grabbed Olivia by the hair and berated Beatriz, subjecting her to a kick. The ordeal continued as they were led into the house, where Olivia received a brutal punishment in the form of hard slaps to both cheeks. She resisted the urge to cry.

"Try that again, and your drunken mother will not live to see her next birthday."

Mrs. George continued, "You think you are a tough little cookie, don't you? Now get back to work, both of you."

Olivia was silent except for a few sniffles and wondered how they had tracked down her mother. Beatriz touched her swollen and red face, and Olivia winced. Yolanda brought her a glass of water as Mrs. George left the room. "Please don't do that again. They will beat me too."

Olivia shook her head, drank the water, and washed her wounds. She was ordered to get to work immediately.

Yolanda saw Mr. George talking to his wife and discreetly listened to their conversation.

"Doesn't she know her mum was arrested? We can't touch her." said Mr. George.

"No, and she better not find out from you or anyone else in this house. And don't worry, I have people watching her. No one gets away from me," his wife replied.

Yolanda looked away.

Harry sat on the edge of his sister Bridgete's bed, gazing at her thoughtfully. She was his only family and, as fate would have it, she also held half of the family's considerable wealth. Harry had always been motivated by money, and his sister's inheritance was a tantalizing prospect. However, he knew he had to maintain a close and amicable relationship with her to ensure he remained in her good graces and she didn't give her wealth away to some stupid animal charity.

They engaged in a casual conversation about her aspirations and where she wished to live. Harry feigned interest while his mind was consumed by thoughts of his girlfriend waiting for him. The nurse's arrival interrupted their conversation, bringing in the evening meal. The nurse, an attractive brunette with large brown eyes, immediately caught Harry's attention. He couldn't help but give her an appraising look from head to toe, a gesture that he assumed might go unnoticed. To his surprise, the nurse didn't seem perturbed by his gaze. She smiled at him and fussed with the bed blankets for a moment before quietly exiting the room.

Unbeknownst to his sister, Harry's calculating mind was already at work, formulating plans and schemes to ensure he not only maintained a hold on his sister's affections but also found a way to secure her inheritance for himself.

Hidden from Harry's view, the nurse discreetly took out her mobile phone. "He's here," she reported.

"Thanks, Agent Roberts. Good work. Now, get the hell out of there," replied Agent Johnson urgently. "I'll notify the agents assigned to tail him."

Agent Johnson walked over to Charles' desk and informed him that they had tracked down Harry. "We have a tail on him as we speak."

Charles struggled to focus on his work, his concentration constantly interrupted by the nagging thought that Harry might be on the verge of getting caught. An hour later, Agent Johnson called him to his office. "Charles, we have an address for Harry, and I've authorized you and Agent McCallum on a two-day surveillance operation."

Charles and Agent McCallum left the agency and signed out

a gray, non-descript van that was equipped with advanced communication and tracking technology. They had been sitting in the van for almost an hour when Charles jokingly said, "I suppose I should go buy coffee and donuts."

McCallum tapped his belly and said, "Sure, I have room for a couple more."

"I was joking," said Charles.

McCallum stared at him, his face serious, "Never joke about food."

They burst out laughing as Charles left to do the coffee errand.

Harry never left his house, and the attractive woman, assumed to be his live-in girlfriend, made occasional outings, returning with shopping bags from Rodeo Drive. A lady, most likely the maid, also made daily trips to the grocery store. The operation to gather information on Harry had hit a roadblock, and Charles knew that they needed a breakthrough soon.

Agent Johnson had earned a reputation over his twenty-five years in the agency as a strict enforcer of the rules. He was known to have terminated a couple of agents in the past for not adhering to protocol. However, in recent times, he had started to show a bit more flexibility in his approach. He understood the complexities of law enforcement and recognized that, at times, agents might need to bend or even break a rule to capture a criminal. The ever-increasing prowess of clever lawyers often allowed criminals to evade justice, and Agent Johnson was becoming more willing to look the other way when a rule violation led to catching a dangerous offender.

After two days, despite the agency's decision to pull the detail due to the lack of progress, Agent Johnson made no objection to Charles' decision to keep surveillance on Harry in his own time. Charles continued his surveillance efforts, knowing that patience and persistence would eventually pay off.

After two more exhausting and uneventful nights, he observed Harry leaving his residence and followed him. This led him to a secluded mansion situated in a remote area. The mansion was surrounded by meticulously maintained gardens, and cameras were strategically placed. Charles kept a safe distance as he peered through his binoculars when he observed a blue van being loaded with long, wooden boxes. His experience told him that they likely contained contraband, possibly firearms. Before returning to his car, his attention was captured by a small figure emerging from the mansion, carrying out the trash. To his shock, it was Olivia. The discovery sent a jolt of urgency through Charles, and he knew that he needed to act carefully and swiftly to ensure Olivia's safety.

29

Charles couldn't contain his restlessness as he paced back and forth in the room, consumed by a mixture of anxiety and determination. Agent Johnson didn't mince words when he snapped at him to calm down and focus on the task at hand. They were dealing with professionals, and any misstep could jeopardize the mission.

"I know," Charles responded with a deep breath, attempting to regain his composure. "But the thought of little Olivia, and who knows how many other kids, stuck in that damn place, it pisses me off. These people can't get away with this crap. I want to stop them and stop them for good."

Despite his impatience, Charles understood the importance of meticulous planning for the impending raid. Lives were at stake, and his primary concern was ensuring Olivia's safety and reuniting her with Sarah. Just two days earlier, Charles had successfully followed the van from the mansion and with the assistance of his team had apprehended the driver, Jerry. It hadn't taken much persuasion to get the information out of the captured man. He had told them there were four armed guards outside, but he wasn't sure how many were inside.

Agent Johnson took charge, assigning positions for all the agents. Time was of the essence, and the plan was finalized, with he himself leading the team. Charles knew that this operation held particular significance for Agent Johnson, who typically remained behind a desk. Since arriving in Los Angeles, the urgency of the situation had driven him to take a hands-on approach.

With positions assigned and the plan finalized by early afternoon, they set off. A small caravan of cars parked out of sight from the surveillance cameras while the blue van, now carrying armed agents, approached the front gates of the mansion. The man posing as the driver was an experienced undercover agent who definitely looked the part, his earwig expertly concealed by his long hair.

Charles listened attentively to the conversation between the agent and Mrs. George as they exchanged pleasantries. "I haven't seen you before; are you new?" Mrs. George inquired.

"Yeah," the agent replied in character. "I'm Vincenzo, Jerry's nephew. He's sick, so I'm just helping for now."

Mrs. George scrutinized him for a moment before instructing, "Take the van around back, and we'll load it there."

Charles watched intently as the van turned the corner, following Mrs. George's directions. As expected, she reached for her phone, and Charles immediately radioed the agent who was holding Jerry, the captured driver. "Get ready for the call," he whispered urgently.

After a brief conversation with Jerry, Mrs. George hung up, seemingly satisfied, and retreated into the mansion. The pieces of the plan were falling into place, and the operation was in motion. Meanwhile, Agent Johnson clicked his radio to communicate an urgent message to the team. "Be extra careful; these people have no qualms about shooting anyone," he warned. Turning to the rest of the team, he shouted, "Now, go, go, go!"

With that command, agents assigned to various positions sprang into action. Some raced around the corner to remain out of sight from any surveillance cameras. Others swiftly entered the mansion, aware that their presence would be detected by the security system. Before any alarm could be raised, one of the agents forcefully kicked down the door of the guard's room, incapacitated the operator, and silenced him with a gag.

Outside, two bodyguards patrolled the mansion's perimeter, but they were caught off guard as two FBI agents seemingly appeared out of nowhere and rendered them unconscious. Inside the house, a guard attempted to alert anyone remaining, resulting in shots being fired.

Charles felt sweat pouring down his face and back. While he had participated in many raids during his career, the thought of Olivia being held hostage haunted him. Suddenly, a bullet whizzed past his head, striking an agent in the shoulder. "Agent down!" Charles yelled, his heart thumping hard against his chest. Another bullet found its mark, this time hitting Charles in the leg. He went down, cursing through the pain. Blood trickled down his injured leg, but he gritted his teeth, took a deep breath, and forced himself to get back up, determined to overcome the pain and continue the mission.

Meanwhile, Mrs. George, in a desperate attempt to escape, descended the stairs and zigzagged her way to the study. Before she could reach for her gun, an FBI agent grabbed and restrained her, despite her kicking in resistance.

Mr. George, appearing visibly shaken, descended the stairs behind her with his hands raised. He pleaded for his safety, saying, "Don't shoot. I'm not armed."

Mrs. George glared at him. "You little rat, don't you dare say anything."

"I'm not taking the blame for this. It was all your idea," said Mr. George.

Agent Johnson ordered, "Get her out of here," and then turned his attention to Mr. George, asking, "How many more bodyguards are there?"

"Just three, but they're trying to escape out back."

Two agents cautiously made their way up the stairs. Halfway to the top, they were met with a barrage of bullets. One agent was hit and tumbled back down the stairs while the other one held back. Simultaneously, agents from the side of the house crept up to the second floor and entered through the windows. They unleashed a rapid volley of gunfire, wounding all three bodyguards.

Agent Johnson shouted, "Check the rest of the house."

Charles forgot his pain and kicked down door after door during the search, blood dripping down his leg.

"All clear," one agent reported.

"All clear," another agent confirmed.

Charles' radio clicked, "Hey, Charlie boy, you'd better come to the third floor to see what I've found."

Charles rushed upstairs. Had they found Olivia? He entered a room to find two girls clinging to each other and sobbing. When the agents entered, the girls screamed in fear. Charles approached them gently.

"Who are you?" he asked.

"We work here," the older girl replied. "I'm Beatriz, and this is Yolanda."

"Where's Olivia?" Charles inquired anxiously.

Yolanda looked at him and said, "That *pelirojo* took her before you got here." Charles understood enough Spanish to know

29

that it was a derogatory term for redhead.

He nodded and offered the girls an understanding smile. "Come on, kids. Let's get you out of here."

The two girls were placed in an agent's car and driven to safety. Charles reluctantly headed to the hospital. Although they initially resisted releasing him, he insisted. Thankfully, the bullet hadn't caused severe damage, but he knew eventually he would require further treatment. On his way back to the FBI bureau, Charles checked his personal cell phone and found three missed calls from Sarah. He dreaded delivering the news that Olivia was still missing. In his office, he finally called Sarah. "She wasn't at the mansion, Sarah."

"But that's impossible; you saw her...," Sarah muttered in disbelief.

"I'll call you later, okay?" Charles suggested, receiving no immediate response. "I'm sorry, Sarah. We will find her; I can assure you of that. The team I work with is dedicated. A couple of us got shot, including me."

He heard a muffled "I'm sorry" from the other end of the line. Charles knew that the search for Olivia would continue, and he was determined to bring her home safely. He knew that memories from Sarah's own kidnapping would come to mind. She had endured a lot and was probably wondering how a twelve-year-old girl like Olivia could navigate such a harrowing situation.

It was all just a quick blur. Olivia had been in the middle of cleaning one of the guest bedrooms in the mansion when she was ambushed from behind. A bag had been forcefully placed over her head, her hands tied tightly behind her back, and she had been dragged down the stairs and tossed into the back of a car. The car had driven for a short while before coming to a halt, and Olivia was unceremoniously pulled out of the vehicle.

Inside a shabby office, the man removed the bag from her head, allowing Olivia to finally see her surroundings. Her frail body trembled uncontrollably. Her legs felt weak, and her breathing was reduced to short, gasping breaths. The man with the red hair, whom she had seen once before at the mansion, stood before her. He was clearly unfazed by her distress and pushed her up against some filing cabinets then retied her hands in front of her, causing her skin to chafe and bleed. He took a seat on a battered desk, his intentions unclear to Olivia, who was trapped in a frightening situation.

She knew that she had to tread carefully to avoid any further harm. Fear and confusion swirled within her, and she couldn't help but ask, "Who are you? What do you want?"

"You'll find out soon enough," he replied. With a hint of menace in his tone, he continued, "Okay, I am going to make a video so your friends Sarah and Charles can see I am serious."

"Serious about what?" Olivia pressed, her voice quivering.

"If they don't let me go, you will suffer," he threatened as Olivia sat very still, her eyes brimming with unshod tears.

A light was turned on, and he pointed his phone towards her, warning her not to say a word. Olivia mustered all her strength, sat up straight, and did as she was told. The recording captured her sitting quietly, her young face etched with worry and uncertainty.

It was early evening and Sarah sat on the floor, her exhaustion evident as she held a cup of hot tea in one hand and her phone in the other. Tears welled up in her eyes as she agonized over Olivia's whereabouts.

Suddenly, her phone chimed with an incoming text from Roger. His text read, *Olivia at docks w/man. Red hair. Not sure of building.*

She quickly forwarded the message to Charles, hoping for a breakthrough.

Moments later, Charles called her. "We received a video from Harry. He has Olivia. He said if we let him leave the country, he will tell us where she is."

"Roger said he saw Harry at the docks."

"We know, but there are so many containers and offices there, we need to know the exact location. We're bringing in our IT guy to analyze the video to see if we can figure out exactly which one she's in."

As they waited for their IT expert to work on the video, Charles felt time dragging on. Half an hour passed until a tall man with black glasses entered the room, offering his assistance. Roy directed him, saying, "Sit here."

The IT expert, with a focused gaze, settled into his seat. He clasped his hands together and gave them a sharp crack. He adjusted his posture, then his fingers swiftly danced across the keyboard, the rhythmic clicks echoing in the room as he tirelessly worked on the video, determined to breach the firewall that had been meticulously set up.

Charles had kept up with technology, but the weird symbols flashing across the screen were too much for him to comprehend. Another half-hour passed, and Agent Johnson suggested a coffee break. Charles declined, determined to keep to watch the video again.

A few minutes later, Agent Johnson returned. "Okay, guys, we just received information from Mr. George. Olivia and some other kids are in a building downtown."

Charles clenched his fists in frustration as Roy delivered the news. He had been eager to join them, but Agent Johnson made it clear that he wouldn't be part of the raid. His injured leg and his personal connection to Sarah were valid reasons, but it didn't ease the frustration bubbling within him.

30

As they left, Charles turned his attention back to the video, scrutinizing every detail. Then, something caught his attention. He noticed Olivia twiddling her fingers in a peculiar manner.

The IT expert remarked, "Wow, does this kid know Morse code?"

Charles replied, "I doubt it. Let me call Sarah."

"Hi, Sarah, I don't suppose Olivia knows Morse code?"

"I don't think so. Why?" Sarah inquired.

"On the video, she's moving her fingers, and...," Charles began.

Sarah interrupted excitedly, "Charles, could she be signing? She learned it from her school friend?"

Charles's eyes widened with realization. "Oh, really? I'll get an interpreter right away."

Another twenty agonizing minutes ticked by until the interpreter finally arrived, gracefully introducing herself as Melanie. Taking her seat with a composed demeanor, she studied the video.

"Okay," she said, "this little girl is spelling out a curious name, Boxter."

Charles immediately called Agent Johnson. No response. "That kid is no dummy," said Charles to no one in particular.

He called Sarah again. "The team has a detail going to some address where Mr. George said they were keeping the kids. How accurate is the info from Roger?"

"He's never been wrong so far."

"Okay, I'm going to check out the docks on my own," he said, determined to take matters into his own hands.

"I'm coming with you," said Sarah.

Charles, concerned for her safety, vehemently objected, but Sarah was resolute.

Sarah insisted. "Pick me up, or I go by myself."

After a tense pause, Charles replied, "Okay, I'll pick you up." He realized she wouldn't take no for an answer.

Charles and Sarah maintained a tense silence as they parked a safe distance away from the office warehouses, while they focused on the situation.

The sun was beginning to set over the San Pedro docks, casting a warm, orange glow across the bustling waterfront. Sarah and Charles sat in the car, gazing out at the sea of cargo containers and towering cranes, trying to pinpoint their destination—a particular building hidden somewhere in this labyrinth of commerce. Charles dialed his boss's number, hoping for backup and assistance in their search. However, he reached voicemail. A few minutes later, his phone beeped, signaling a text message. The response he received left him frustrated. Agent Johnson dismissed his information without a second thought. "Charles, I know you have a personal interest in this case, but we have to go with the information we got from Mr. George. He is our most reliable witness."

Charles turned to Sarah, "Agent Johnson insists we are on a wild goose chase."

Sarah responded firmly, her faith in Olivia evident. "I don't care. Look at the video. Olivia is so smart."

"Okay, keep your head down and stay in the car," Charles instructed. "As long as we're here, I'm gonna check out this place."

Despite his boss's skepticism, Charles couldn't let go of the hope that their lead might be the right one. He entered an empty office that appeared to serve as a reception area and scanned his surroundings. There was no one in sight, but he spotted a list of businesses occupying various buildings in the area. With a sense of urgency, he carefully scrolled through it. "Nothing, damn it!" he muttered in frustration, as Boxter was not listed. He returned to the car and informed Sarah of his plan. "Sarah, we need to look around. The name is probably not showing, as whoever owns it wants to keep a low profile."

As they began to navigate through the maze of cargo containers stacked like giant Lego blocks, the sounds of machinery, distant ship horns, and the rhythmic clatter of forklifts filled the air. Seagulls circled overhead, providing an occasional raucous soundtrack. They saw several office spaces. Charles spotted a building devoid of a name, an ominous sign that piqued his interest. "There's a building with no name," he told Sarah. "Stay here and stay low. Don't leave the car."

Charles carefully approached the dirty brown door and reached for the handle, but it wouldn't budge. He pushed it with his shoulder and it creaked open. He drew his firearm. The interior was shrouded in darkness and silence. He strained to hear any signs of life or movement. With each step he took, the old floorboards protested, creaking loudly beneath his feet. Dust particles floated in the air, catching the faint light that seeped through cracked windows. The silence was broken by the slamming of the door, which sent a shiver down his spine.

He tightened his grip on his firearm and returned to the door. *Did the wind blow it shut or did someone slam it closed?*

Back in the car, Sarah anxiously followed Charles's movements from her low vantage point. She felt for his safety and admired his determination. *Hopefully, when this is all over...* her thoughts were interrupted, and her heart pounded as she peered through the car window and saw a figure emerge from the adjacent office, heading toward the building Charles had just entered. She grabbed her phone. It rang. But Charles' phone was on the seat. "Shit, Charles, you forgot your damn phone." She cursed under her breath as she watched the intruder lock the door where Charles had entered and retreat into the neighboring office.

Sarah felt a growing sense of desperation, unsure of what to do next. Then, her worst fears were realized as she saw two figures emerge—one of them was Olivia. The sight of her being held by Harry sent Sarah's panic into overdrive.

"Ow, you're hurting me," Olivia's frightened voice reached Sarah's ears, causing her heart to ache.

"Shut up, or I'll hurt you even more," said Harry.

The sound of Olivia's voice gave Sarah the courage she needed to muster her strength. She cautiously exited the car and scanned her surroundings. She spotted a piece of wood nearby. Silently, she picked it up, gripping it tightly as the adrenaline coursed through her veins. She began to sneak along the edge of the building, following the voices. As she turned a corner, she jumped, finding herself face to face with Harry, who was brandishing a gun. "One false move, and you'll find a bullet in your leg."

Without thinking, she reached for Olivia, but Harry hit her

30

with the butt of his gun. She let out a terrified scream, and collapsed to the ground. At the same a gunshot went off.

Harry, dragging Olivia towards his car, was momentarily distracted by the gunshot. It didn't come from his gun. In that moment, Olivia managed to break free from his grasp and sprinted back to Sarah's fallen form.

"Wake up, wake up," Olivia pleaded desperately, throwing herself onto Sarah's chest.

Harry grabbed her once gain.

31

The shot that rang out had indeed come from Charles's gun as he aimed at the lock on the door. The sound of the bullet ricocheting and echoing through the empty warehouse was deafening. As he fired, he heard something stir inside. A frightened cat darted past him, clutching a tiny mouse in its jaws. Charles was desperate. He had heard the scratchy voice of Harry Whelan and the trembling, high-pitched voice of Sarah. He couldn't waste a moment. With the lock finally broken, he flung the door open. He saw Harry, armed, and he was holding Olivia too close for him to take a shot. He raised his voice in a desperate plea, "Let her go, Harry. It's me you want, not them."

In response, something struck the wall nearby with a loud thud, followed by a rain of rocks and stones pelting the area around Charles. He swiftly moved to the side, trying to shield himself from the onslaught of projectiles. Amidst the chaos, Charles saw Sarah on the ground and watched Harry fall. Olivia ran towards Sarah. The barrage of flying rocks gradually subsided, revealing a group of ragged children fleeing the scene, holding fiercely onto their homemade catapults. Without hesitation, Charles sprinted over to Harry. Ignoring the injuries on his face, he swiftly handcuffed and hog-tied him before securing him in the back of a car. He couldn't afford to take any chances.

Carefully, he leaned over Sarah and gently lifted her, placing her in the front seat of the car with Olivia beside her. His face was pale with worry as he said to Olivia, "Come on, let's get her to the hospital." Charles hoped and prayed that Sarah's injuries were not severe, but he knew they needed medical attention urgently. He quickly called his boss and informed him that he was taking Sarah to the hospital and requested backup to pick up Harry. "Olivia is with us," he added.

"Shit," came Agent Johnson's response. "I guess Mr. George was wrong about Olivia, but he did make a deal with the District Attorney, and now we have all the addresses of the other residences where they have child labor. We're on our way now."

"You do know Harry Whelan was behind all of this?" said Charles.

"Yup!" replied his boss, "He got smart. This is not a trafficking ring from Mexico. These bastards hang out in local spots right here in California and look for drug addicts who have children, then offer them money and drugs in exchange for their child."

Charles couldn't believe the depths of depravity involved in this operation, and he clenched his fists in anger. There was much work to be done to dismantle this network and get those responsible locked up.

Sarah's head no longer throbbed with pain, and she felt an overwhelming sense of peace. She wondered if this was heaven, as she had heard people describe a bright white light in such moments. She moaned softly and then heard a voice she recognized—Olivia's.

"Sarah, you're alive!" Olivia exclaimed.

Charles lent over her and held her hand, "You're safe now. How do you feel?"

Sarah blinked in the harsh, fluorescent light of the hospital room and looked around, feeling somewhat disoriented. "Well, at one point, I thought I was in heaven," she replied, then smiled. Tears welled up in her eyes as Olivia hugged her tightly.

Sarah reluctantly released Olivia, who picked up her new phone. As a bonus, the FBI had kindly bought her a smartphone. "Wow, I have so many messages. All my friends think it's so cool what happened," said Olivia.

Sarah rolled her eyes, then turned to Charles, eager to understand what had happened.

"You have some very unusual friends," he said.

Confused, Sarah inquired, "What do you mean?"

"Those kids. They must have been the band of kids that Roger hung out with."

"Why, what happened?"

"You told me you wanted to get them off the streets for their own safety. No need. I reckon they are doing quite well on their own. After Harry had knocked you out; I must admit I was surprised he didn't shoot you, they came down and pelted hundreds of rocks at him. Those kids managed to knock Harry Whelan down, which gave me the chance to tie up that bastard."

"That's funny. I guess Roger will send me a bill. They're all street kids, runaways. Roger seems to be the leader. The whole situation reminded me of *Oliver Twist*."

Charles chuckled, "Roger the Dodger!" then, as he stood up, he grimaced in pain from his gunshot wound.

Sarah's eyes widened, "Is your gunshot wound still bothering you?"

"A little."

Sarah looked around the private room. "This is a very nice room. Will they be sending me a bill?"

"No, don't worry. The FBI figured you deserved a reward for your help, even though Agent Johnson is still mad at me for involving you. You are here until the doctor assures us that you don't have a concussion." He paused slightly. "There's something else I have to tell you. Olivia's mother was arrested because of what she did to Olivia and could spend a very long time in prison. Sarah's brow furrowed. "I'll have to tell Olivia. She did love her mother in a way, or maybe she just felt responsible, or maybe even felt sorry for her."

"Yes, but she's a strong kid, she'll be able to handle the news," said Charles.

"So, I still have some unanswered questions," said Sarah. "Especially from when I was in Mexico."

"Remember when we were at the ruins?" said Charles.

"How can I forget?"

"We were being followed because Carmen had informed Manuel about the suspicion that you had taken the drugs."

"Well," said Sarah, "I guess that's why they kept asking me about *zee* package."

Sarah's accent brought a moment of levity to their conversation, and they both broke into laughter.

"Then, when your room was ransacked, they were hoping to find your phone. One of the photos I took at the ruins, had inadvertently captured one of Manuel's men in the background, and they were hoping to retrieve it."

A soft knock echoed on the door. "Come in," invited Sarah.

Anne entered, gracefully bearing a sizable bowl of grapes. She placed it on the table and leaned in gently to plant a tender kiss on Sarah's cheek.

"Okay," said Charles, "You are in good hands. I'll leave you two to catch up." He kissed Sarah on the cheek and whispered, "I'll call you later."

Anne was full of questions, and Sarah recounted what had happened up to the point she blacked out.

The doctor entered, carrying a clipboard. Sarah noticed her perfect olive skin and beautiful, sleek black hair pulled back in a tight bun. "We checked everything, and it's okay for you to stay another day or go home, your choice," she said.

"Thank you, doctor. I think I would like to go home."

As the doctor left, another visitor arrived. It was JW, carrying a large bouquet of flowers.

"Hello. What a pleasant surprise," said Sarah.

"How are you?"

"Getting better by the minute."

He placed the flowers on the table and asked if he should get a vase from the nurse.

"No, I'm getting discharged today, so I'll take them home."

Anne regarded him with a blend of curiosity and desire. His features, kissed by the sun, exuded a dark allure. Clad in a pair of well-fitted jeans and a polo shirt, he exuded a casual yet magnetic presence.

"Anne!" Sarah playfully made a face at her then turned to JW, "This is my assistant Anne."

"Oh, sorry. Aren't you the reporter from channel six?" stammered Anne.

JW extended his hand, and Anne shook it fervently. "Okay, Sarah, I better get back to the office. Mrs. Robertson is on her way. She wants another cruise organized." she said, slightly embarrassed at her reaction to JW. She said goodbye to them all and hurried through the door.

"Thanks," said Sarah, calling after her. "I should be back in the office on Monday."

JW turned his attention to Olivia, "So, you're the one all this fuss was about?"

Olivia took her eyes off her phone and giggled. "Yeah. Are you famous?" she asked innocently.

"Yes," he joked, "Do you want my autograph?"

"Nah! I've never seen you in any movies," she said and immediately returned to her text messages.

Sarah and JW laughed. "Olivia, please take your eyes off that phone, or I may take it from you."

"Sarah, how about helping me write this story?" asked JW. "You too, Olivia."

Olivia looked over, her eyes wide, "Do you mean I could be on TV?"

"Maybe."

"Cool."

"Olivia, I heard that you were very brave, so I have a surprise for you," said JW with a twinkle in his eye.

"What is it?" asked Olivia, her excitement palpable.

"Well, it wouldn't be a surprise if I told you," JW replied with a playful grin. "I'll call Sarah and let her know when and where. Is that okay with you, Sarah?"

"Sure," replied Sarah, her eyebrows furrowing in a quizzical look as she wondered what JW had up his sleeve.

"Until then," said JW, as he turned to leave.

32

After JW left, Sarah was discharged. The nurse entered her room and insisted that she was escorted to the exit in a wheelchair.

"I'm fine," Sarah protested, "I can manage."

"Hospital rules," said the nurse gruffly as she put her hand on Sarah's shoulder.

With Olivia by her side, they rolled through the stark hallways of the hospital to the exit, where a taxi was waiting for them. They climbed in and sat back, glad to be on their way home. Olivia peeked over the bouquet of flowers and laughed. She looked at Sarah and said, "I wish you had told them to take you home in an ambulance. I've never been in one."

"Nor have I," said Sarah, "and I don't intend to ever be in one."

Sarah released a heavy sigh as she turned the key in the lock of her condo, feeling the weight of recent events bearing down upon her shoulders. Olivia scampered off to find a vase for the flowers while Sarah busied herself filling the kettle. "Now for a decent cup of tea," she muttered to herself. Settling onto the sofa, she cradled the mug in her hands, the steam rising soothingly, and Olivia snuggled up beside her.

Sarah's thoughts swirled through her head. The kidnapping,

the FBI, Charles showing up, Harry arriving in the US, and the scene at the docks. She felt lucky that no serious harm had come to any of them. The phone rang. It was Charles.

"How are you? I'm surprised you left the hospital so soon."

"I'm fine," said Sarah.

"I was thinking," said Charles, "Would you be up to having dinner with me tomorrow evening?"

Sarah hesitated before replying. "Okay, what time?"

"I'll pick you up at eight, if that suits you."

Sarah agreed and put down the phone. She found herself grappling with a whirlwind of emotions regarding Charles. Reflecting on their time together, she contemplated the stark difference between the exhilarating adventures they had experienced in Mexico and the unsettling events that unfolded in the US. A wry chuckle escaped her lips as she contemplated the inevitable return to the mundane realities of how their lives would be in the near future. In comparison to the whirlwind of events they had currently experienced, she knew that the everyday challenges would seem trivial by comparison.

However, was she ready for a relationship? Was Charles really ready?

Sarah and Olivia slept late. It was the best sleep they had had in several weeks. Sarah's head ached a little but cleared up after a hefty breakfast and two cups of coffee. It was a Saturday, so Sarah asked Olivia what she wanted to do. Surprisingly she answered, "I have so much homework to do before Monday, so I ain't going nowhere."

Sarah was about to correct her grammar but stopped. It sounded kind of cute coming from Olivia. Sarah checked her laptop for messages while Olivia buried herself in her schoolbooks.

While Sarah was getting dressed, Olivia went to the wardrobe and picked out a dress. "You should wear this one."

"Oh, really. Are you my stylist? Actually it was a choice between that one and this one," she said holding up another dress. "But I think your choice is best." Sarah sat on the bed and motioned for Olivia to join her. "Olivia I have to tell you something about your mom." Sarah explained the situation.

"Olivia looked at Sarah, a little teary eyed and said, "Well, maybe she will be better in there. She can get off drugs and maybe learn a new job. I heard that some prisoners become lawyers and stuff."

Sarah smiled, impressed by Olivia's maturity. Maybe she was right, but Sarah knew drugs were rampant in prisons.

At eight p.m. promptly, there was a knock on the door. Sarah peeked through the peephole out of habit and saw Charles. She opened the door, and he was armed with a huge bouquet of flowers. "I couldn't be outdone by that handsome journalist," he said.

They waited a few minutes until Anne arrived as Sarah still didn't want to leave Olivia on her own. Sarah kissed Olivia and left with Charles. "I rented a car so we could have a leisurely drive."

The fiery sun was just disappearing behind the horizon as they drove to Malibu. As the road twisted and turned, she caught glimpses of the calm ocean. Thirty minutes later, they arrived at Beau Rivage, a restaurant Sarah had visited only a few times but always recommended to her high-end clients. It was a warm evening, so they sat at a round table outside. Fairy lights twinkled in all the surrounding trees. It was a place many celebrities frequented, so she remembered a few years ago seeing Julie Andrews, and another time, Michael Caine. She looked around casually but didn't spot any celebs, at least not ones she would recognize.

"Charles, thank you. I really love this place. I'm surprised you knew about it."

Charles smiled as the waiter pulled out her chair, placed the napkin on her lap and handed her the menu. Charles asked Sarah if she wanted an aperitif.

"Thanks, but a couple glasses of wine will suit me fine." The waiter returned with the wine that Charles had chosen and spouted out the specials.

They both started with lobster bisque and for the entree, Sarah chose Dover sole meunière, while Charles decided on the filet mignon Rossini. Charles looked very handsome, and they chatted comfortably. After the main course, Charles took her hand in his and said, "Sarah, I've been thinking about you a lot. If I decide to stay in the US, I was thinking of buying a house in Long Beach."

"Oh! I thought this move was already permanent."

"Well, I wanted to make sure that this job and life was really for me, so I haven't made any definite plans."

Sarah hoped he wasn't making the move because of her. She didn't want that responsibility. After all, she was still undecided about her feelings for him.

"I want to know if you still have feelings for me. Enough for you and Olivia to move in with me. No pressure. But I think you already know how I feel."

Sarah withdrew her hand, perhaps a touch too abruptly, and stumbled over her words.

"Oh, Charles, I... I don't know. With everything that's been happening lately, I feel like I need to focus on being there for

Olivia and myself. I appreciate your honesty, but I just don't know how I feel yet. I mean, you're amazing, but I'm still trying to figure things out."

"Of course you are. And whatever happens, I'm here for you," said Charles.

"That means a lot. Let's just take things one step at a time, okay?" She felt terrible, and she couldn't bear to meet Charles's gaze as she sensed his disappointment. His smile had vanished, replaced by an expression of silent dismay. He parted his lips as if to speak, but no words emerged. The silence was deafening. Sarah looked at him and said, "I will definitely think about it, as I do like you a lot."

"Well, that's a start," said Charles, "I'm a patient man."

After the main course, they enjoyed a big bowl of strawberry ice cream then chatted a little more until Sarah let out a wide yawn. "Sorry, I'm a little tired. Can we go home now?"

Sarah went to the ladies room as Charles paid the bill. She stared at her image in the mirror. *Oh! God, I'm so confused.* She splashed her face with cold water, combed her hair, took a deep breath, and met Charles at the exit. The valet pulled up in the car and opened the passenger door for Sarah. They drove back in silence. Outside her condo, Charles said, "Please think about this carefully. I do love you."

"Okay," she said as she planted a gentle kiss on his cheek.

Sarah was greeted with an enthusiastic hug from Olivia and a quizzical stare from Anne. "You're back early."

"Yes, I was tired."

"Okay," said Anne surreptitiously. "I'll see you Monday."

"How's your studying?" asked Sarah to Olivia.

"Pfuff. I've had enough. My eyes hurt. I'm going to bed." She kissed Sarah goodnight and walked to her room.

"Goodnight, sweetheart. See you in the morning."

Sarah woke at ten when the phone rang. It was JW. "Good morning, beautiful. Do you have anything planned for today?"

"No," replied Sarah sleepily.

"Okay, why don't you and Olivia get ready, and I'll pick you up in an hour."

"Where are we going? What do we wear?"

"Nothing fancy, stay casual." He hung up.

Sarah called Olivia. They showered and dressed. Sarah downed a coffee quickly while Olivia drank her juice and scoffed down a waffle.

JW picked them up. "Can I call you Johnny?" Sarah asked.

"Sure," he replied.

"Where are we going?"

"I told you both, it's a surprise."

As they pulled up in front of the towering building adorned with gleaming letters spelling out Starview Studios, Olivia screamed with excitement. She was well aware that this company was the creative force behind her favorite show, *Enchanted Grove Gang*, a thrilling series centered around a group of adventurous kids turned detectives.

Sarah looked at JW and said, "How did you know Olivia liked this show?"

"I heard her talking about it when I was visiting you in hospital."

Olivia's eyes were brimming with anticipation as they stepped through the grand entrance of the TV studios. The air hummed with an electric energy. Sarah watched her as she looked around at all the people bustling about, checking cameras, and sets being meticulously arranged. Olivia gave JW a big hug as she realized she was standing in the very heart of the studio that brought her favorite shows to life.

"They just finished their final rehearsal, and now it's time to tape it, so let's sit," said JW.

They sat in three seats in the front row, which apparently had been reserved for them. The crew prepared for a full day of filming. Brightly colored sets created a fantastical backdrop for the show's young stars. As the cameras rolled, the cast, dressed in vibrant costumes, brought their characters to life with infectious energy and enthusiasm. Behind the scenes, the director called out instructions while technicians worked tirelessly to ensure every detail was perfect. Amidst the controlled chaos, laughter filled the air as the audience enjoyed the actors' banter in between scenes. The studio had been transformed into a playground of imagination, where adventures unfolded before the eager eyes of young viewers everywhere. It took almost three hours to tape the thirty-minute episode.

When it finished, Olivia said dryly, "I thought I wanted to be an actor, and it looks like fun, but it's just not that glamorous. All that starting and stopping. I just wouldn't have the patience."

Sarah and JW laughed. "Do you want to stay for the next episode?" asked JW.

"Er... nope. I'm hungry," replied Olivia.

JW looked at Sarah and said, "I thought this would cheer her up after all the drama.

"Thanks," said Sarah, "It was a wonderful idea."

They left the studios, walked to a local diner, and ate hamburgers accompanied by a large portion of fries, then washed it down with a strawberry milkshake. Sarah had to admit she was pleasantly surprised by how JW interacted with Olivia. At first, she thought he was just another overconfident guy trying to impress everyone, but watching him today was like seeing a whole different side to him. She could see why Olivia liked him. He was genuine, caring, and he really listened to her. She didn't even think that he was trying to impress her, just being a good friend.

She sat silently on the way home as JW and Olivia chatted. Her thoughts kept going back to Charles. Her feelings had become blurred since leaving Mexico. She did like him, but did she love him? Would she rather just spend time with Olivia and have a few casual dates until she knew in her own mind what she really wanted?

They arrived back at the condo. JW had to go on an assignment, so he kissed her gently on the cheek, gave Olivia a hug, and said goodbye. Sarah waved as he drove off, then walked through the garden to her front door. The familiar click of her key in the lock was accompanied by a sudden noise, jolting her nerves into overdrive. Sarah's senses sharpened, her stomach twisted with unease, and her heart pounded. Instinctively, she flung the door open and urgently called out to Olivia to go inside. Memories of her past kidnapping flooded her mind, igniting a primal fear within her. Fumbling in her bag, she retrieved a canister of mace, ready to defend herself. But as she turned, her eyes widened in surprise as she saw a raccoon scavenging through the overturned garbage bin. That was an unusual sight as they were normally nocturnal creatures. She let out a nervous laugh as the tension drained from her body. *When will this nervousness dissipate? Should I take self-defense classes? Should I speak to a psychiatrist? I now have a child to protect.* She went inside, threw off her shoes, and sank onto the sofa. She grabbed Olivia, who was oblivious to Sarah's nervousness, and gave her a tight hug.

"What was that for?" said Olivia.

"Can't I just hug you when I feel like it?"

"Yeah, I guess," said Olivia, "You can hug me anytime, but can I finish texting my friends now? They'll all be so jealous."

Sarah couldn't help but smile as she observed Olivia's fingers dance across the phone keypad, recounting the day's events to her friends. The sight filled her with warmth as she thought about what they had been through together. It was moments like these that reminded Sarah of the simple joys of motherhood, and she cherished every precious second of it.

Now, Sarah knew in her heart that she would be very happy with only Olivia by her side. As she sat in her pensive mood, she knew the answer to Charles' proposition.

About the Author

Anna Alcott was born in Newcastle upon Tyne, in the UK. She has always had the travel bug, and after living in Blackpool and London, eventually moved overseas. She lived in Italy, Spain, Lebanon, Saudi Arabia, The Bahamas, Jamaica, Canada and the US. She returned to Cornwall, in the UK for five years but couldn't handle the cold weather, so after a few months in Greece, now resides in Portugal with her feline companion.

You can connect with me on:
- https://www.annaalcott.com
- https://www.facebook.com/groups/834381758466910
- https://www.instagram.com/anna.alcott

Subscribe to my newsletter:
- https://us3.admin.mailchimp.com

Also by Anna Alcott

The adventures of Zoe Hunter
Zoe Hunter leaves her small home town for London to pursue her dreams of becoming a dancer. Based on true events from 1968 to 1984. This will entertain those who have grown up without social media, while offering an insight to those who are familiar with its pervasive presence.

Cover Design: SelfPubBookCovers.com/litberry